The BRIDGE

By Jeri Massi

Bob Jones University Press, Greenville, South Carolina 29614

The Bridge

Edited by Richard Barry

Cover and illustrations by Stephanie True

©1986 by Bob Jones University Press
Greenville, South Carolina 29614

ISBN 0-89084-348-1
Printed in the United States of America

20   19   18   17   16   15   14   13   12   11   10   9   8

For Marie Bayer

The Bracken Trilogy

The Bridge
Crown and Jewel
The Two Collars

CONTENTS

CONTENTS

1
Escape at Night

Come war, the soldier earns his trade.
Beat the drums; my heart inspire.
Bring me my iron blade,
My helmet rivet on.
Bring me the prancing horse.
Gird on my sword of fire.

Nay, come there many boots,
On cobblestones that ring?
Disarm me where the waters course.
My iron helm unhinge.
A riverboat shall be my horse.
One axe shall overthrow a king.

In the night the soldier creeps,
Midway from shore to shore.
High above the murky deep
He finds a slender wooden floor.
'Twill one man safely keep,
Whose axe shall end a war.

Long ago a river divided two kingdoms—one great and one small. The large kingdom was Folger, with a fullness to its name that sounded out the fullness of its boundaries. The small kingdom, like the bric-a-brac along the shelf, was called Bracken.

Now the King of Bracken rode to attend his brother's fox hunt, and the King left his daughter Rosalynn in care of his most trusted knight, Sir Reynald.

And even as the King of Bracken went out to hunt in sport, Lord Rigel, master of Folger, went to hunt in earnest. He set his heart to swallow up the little kingdom and slay every royal person down to the Princess herself.

Now Rigel of Folger was broad. He stood no higher than a horse's shoulder, but he was so wide with muscle that he could actually tear young trees from the ground, a sport he found entertaining when he was out riding. Wily as a fox he was, and sharp as a knife, but for all his shrewdness, he could not make his land produce crops. Forest he had in abundance along his side of the river, overflowing with trees. But his fields were poor, as though the ground itself rebelled against so barbaric a ruler as he.

So the wicked king laid his plans for the complete and utter takeover of Bracken, and his plans fell so that he would attack the moment night fell on that first day of the first month of spring.

But to Sir Reynald, thoughts of battle were distant, like the blurry horizon line. Wars had long since ceased. The only entrance way to Bracken was over the Bridge that spanned the river, and Bracken soldiers guarded it day and night, so that for fifteen long years the hungry armies of Folger had been stilled. Even though the

Folgerians outnumbered the Bracken soldiers, only ten men could cross the Bridge side by side together, so a small force on the Bracken side could have stood off the entire forces of Folger. Bracken's safety hung on being alerted to enemies on the Bridge.

In this time of peace few suspected an attack. Reynald, a knight with many battles in the distant past, kept sentries posted along the pathways to the Bridge. But he worried little. The two nations were at peace.

In the early afternoon he walked with her little majesty through the garden and out past the stables to the patch where wild strawberries grew.

"Oh, Reynald, let me go riding with you," Princess Rosalynn begged him that afternoon. "Put me in front on your great saddle and ride with me."

"Nay, my lady," he said, smiling at her as fondly as any beloved uncle would have done. "My poor horse is old, like I am. He wants his oats right now. Maybe later we can ride."

"You know that you aren't old," she retorted. "It's untruth to say it. Your hair's not even white yet."

"Little majesty, you mustn't rebuke your subject so. I'm old enough." He swept her off her feet to make her laugh and swung her in a circle with one arm. But as he spun toward the north he felt a chill, and his eyes scanned the horizon hungrily. Some telltale sign had struck a deep note in him, warning him of danger. Even he wasn't sure what it was. But there was something in that late afternoon sky that he hadn't seen before. "I will take you to your supper," he said at last. Then he noticed what was troubling him. The birds that normally roosted in the forest along the river were winging their way over fields and meadows in search of new roosting places.

His keen soldier's eye saw that something had disturbed them—some great hubbub crossing over the Bridge into the forest. And his heart suddenly beat coldly with a suspicion. For it takes great noise and great numbers to frighten away the birds from a forest.

He hurried into the great house with her. "Stay in the kitchen with your nurse," he told her. He handed her into the care of the old servant who had been mother to Rosalynn since the Queen's death.

The knight hurried forward to the courtyard and up the battlements to scan the fringe of trees on the far side of the fields. To be sure he saw only a lone sentry riding pell-mell for the gate.

"Muster the men!" he ordered quickly to his captain. "Sound the alarm, and prepare to close the gates!"

Trumpeters quickly blared the warning. From below, horses neighed in protest as they were driven out for saddling. Men shouted; peasants from the neighboring fields hallooed to each other and came running. And all the while the sentry in the distance drove his horse on as a man insane, bent forward for the castle.

"The castle guard is summoned, my leader," the captain told him. Reynald looked down in dismay at a small group of soldiers standing resolute and ready down below.

"Where are the others?"

"Home in the fields, sire. Plowing time is on us. The King spared them to go."

Reynald turned and saw the sentry come riding in, disappearing under the stone archway below as his horse scrambled in to safety. "Close the gate," he ordered. "Have every bowman take his position on the parapet. Bring that sentry to me."

4

"As you wish, sire." The captain raced away to carry out his orders. Moments later, one of the young pages led the exhausted sentry to Reynald.

"Enemies on the Bridge, sir. They quietly slipped in and took the sentries last night in the dark woods. Only I have escaped. I hid in the woods all day for fear of being killed, but at last I took one of their horses and made a dash for the castle. Rigel of Folger himself will ride over the Bridge with a new troop at sunset and storm the castle at last light. Such is what I've overheard from the murderous forward guard."

"Sunset," Reynald said. The sun had already dipped past the line of trees. "Fetch me the King's second-best crown," he told the page who was still standing nearby. "And fetch me the ermine-trimmed robe. Tell the royal valet that the crown and robe are necessary to save the Princess. Show him my ring. Go quickly."

Down below, a half dozen burly gate guards were straining at the huge doors, slowly pulling them in a semicircle until they closed with an echoing slam of mighty oak against solid stone. Immediately twelve men climbed atop the shoulders of twelve of their fellows and sat there. An enormous tree, trimmed of its branches and cut square, was hefted onto the sweating shoulders of men below, then lifted to the men above them. These men, muscles straining, lifted the bar and set it into the great iron tongues that would hold it in place.

Up above, Reynald struggled into the King's robe. He stared at the crown a moment, as though preparing himself for something painful. Then he set it on his head and gave it a slight tug as though it were his helmet.

"I go to the Princess," he told the astonished captain. "Defend the wall. Rigel of Folger takes no prisoners.

We have no choice but to fight. You," he called to the page. "Send Herron the Rider to the kitchen."

Quickly he left the courtyard.

Reynald entered the kitchen where Rosalynn and her nurse were waiting. "Good woman, release me," Rosalynn said to her when she saw Reynald. She pulled herself away from her nurse's arms.

"Explain yourself," she said sharply to Reynald. "Your manner of dressing greatly displeases us. It is treasonous to wear the King's crown and robe."

"Aye, little majesty," he agreed respectfully. "My conduct is shocking and may be wasted in the end. But I hope to serve my king. In this I am clear of guilt."

"Explain yourself," she repeated.

"The castle is under attack. Your father's old enemy, Rigel of Folger, is marching this way to storm the castle. Our circumstances are hopeless, and your life is in great danger. I plan to save you."

"How so? By stealing my father's crown for yourself?" she demanded. Undaunted by his size and sure of her authority, she took a step closer. In all her ten years she had been taught that one day her word would be law, and she feared no person in all her father's realm.

"Guards!" she called. "Seize this imposter!" But nothing happened.

"Nay, little Princess," he said gravely. "Squires!" he called. His squires, three of them, entered from behind him.

"Bring me peasant clothes to fit this child," he said to one of them. "And summon my wife." Then to the Princess he added, "Time is essential, little majesty, and I cannot allow you to order me to stop, nor can I grant you the grace of time to consider my plans. Speed is necessary, and I will spare you the heartbreak of this decision. As regent, I will proceed as I think best."

"By dressing me in peasant clothes for this pretend war of yours?" she demanded. "Never! Guards!"

Still no guards came. "You are a disloyal traitor!" she shrieked, more like a terrified child than a princess. "Take off that crown!"

He remained unmoved, and she started to run out of the kitchen. Just as quickly he raised his hand, and the two remaining squires blocked the doorways.

"Do you yet not see what Rigel would do if he found the royal Princess—" Reynald began.

"Traitor!" she shrieked.

"Your majesty," he began, trying to calm her. "I plead with you to control yourself."

Just then the third squire returned with the clothing and Reynald's wife.

"You must trust me now, Rosalynn," he told her. "My wife will dress you if you do not obey. You are to go to your rooms and remove your royal clothes, wearing instead the clothing of a farm girl."

"No!"

He nodded to the nearest squire. Struggling and screaming, Rosalynn was picked up and carried to her rooms. Reynald turned to his wife. "Do to her as I commanded. Her nurse will help you. I suspect it will take both of you. Spare not for her tears, but work quickly."

They hurried out, following the crying and shouting Princess and the dogged squire carrying her.

"Well done," Reynald said to the other young men. "Go attend the other job on the wall."

Just then Herron the Rider strode in. He wore high brown boots, green leggings, and a loose green tunic with a spacious cowl. Herron was barely eighteen, lean and light as a whip, yet almost as tall as Reynald himself. "You sent for me, my lord?" he asked. Though the whole castle was in a panic to prepare for the impending siege, he carried himself as calmly as though spring plowing were the order for the day.

"Aye," Reynald said. "You alone don't seem surprised at finding me dressed as the King."

"Nay. I see your plan. If the castle falls in battle, the soldiers of that scoundrel, Rigel of Folger, will think they have killed the King of Bracken. It is a good and noble plan." And he gave a quick nod of grim approval.

"You expect nothing less than bravery from yourself and others, Herron," the older knight said. "Yet your task this night is to flee with the Princess to his true majesty with the news of the attack."

"Flying through these woods tonight may have danger enough to settle my stomach. But how can we get out? The gate is barred. As I came in the archers were busy plying their wares. War is now upon us."

"My squires have gone to knock out a part of the south wall and make a hole for a horse to be let out. Then you and the Princess must ride like the wind."

"Aye, liege. Where is her majesty?"

"Upstairs. Being forced into peasant clothes."

"I see." The tall and manly youth's eyebrows went up. "Her majesty dislikes your plans?"

"She has no understanding, Herron. How could I take the time to explain it all to her, and then risk that she would understand and order me to forbear and keep her here? My bones tell me the castle will fall. Rosalynn must escape. So long as there is even a child of the royal family, then Bracken will yet overthrow the yoke of Folger. The people shall stand behind their Princess. And news must reach the King in time."

"Aye." Herron shifted his weight.

"My wife will see that the jewel of royalty is set around her neck and hidden under her garments. Take care that it is not wrenched off. It is her claim to the throne."

"Aye."

"Come, she must be ready by now."

They strode out into the great hall in time to see Rosalynn, now exhausted from her struggles, weeping as she was led down the stairs. Even through the shuttered windows in the hall, shouts from the parapets were drifting inside, and they could hear a muffled *boom! boom!* as a battering ram tested its strength against the sturdy gates.

At sight of Reynald the Princess hung back and glared, but then she saw young Herron the Rider.

"Herron!" she cried, and flung herself into his arms. "Oh, Herron, save me! Look at what they have done to me!"

"There now, my little Princess," he said tenderly. "Have no fear. Your faithful Herron is here, and nobody will hurt you."

"You are still loyal to me then?" she asked, looking up at him.

"Dear and gracious lady," he said, stroking her ruffled and damp curls. "Every man and woman in this room is loyal to you."

"We are ready to die for you!" Reynald insisted, troubled by her terror and hatred of him. She turned her back to him.

"Come!" Herron told her. "I will take you to your father. The castle is under siege, and we must ride swiftly and silently, though night falls around us."

She turned and eyed Sir Reynald, but he was in control of himself again and only looked at her sorrowfully.

"Is this his order?" she asked suspiciously.

Instead of answering directly, Herron said, "It is my own fondest wish to deliver my Princess from the jaws of danger. Will you come with me, dear Princess Rosalynn? Once we are out of danger, I will even let you hold the reins, and I have sugar that you can feed my horse, Javelin—if he doesn't frighten you."

Speech like this was more to the Princess's liking. "Yes, I will go with you, Herron," she said, smoothing down her rough peasant dress with great dignity. "Please take me to my father."

"Aye, little majesty." He took her hand and led her out. Reynald followed.

At first it was a great comfort to walk hand in hand with the handsome and loyal Herron. But all around the north wall, where the gate was, the men were sweating and shooting and toiling in earnest, and huge torches were being lit, guttering and sputtering. Above all there rose a burning smell and a smell of sweat, fear, and terrible earnestness. Resolutely, he led her back to the south wall, with Reynald a short distance behind. The sky was lowering, the grounds growing darker as the sun slid away behind the western walls.

"See there," Herron said as they saw the young men hacking at the wall with pickaxes and hammers. "We will lead Javelin out that hole and escape."

"Oh, Herron," she said, and looked up.

"Yes, Princess?"

"They have taken my queenly garments and given me peasant clothes. And now I am taken away secretly. No one outside these walls would know I am the Princess. Promise me you are not going to take me out into the forest to kill me. I have read of stories like this in my storybooks. Promise me this isn't your plan."

"Why, Rosalynn!" He was truly shocked. "I mean, your majesty, may I be hanged if ever I had the thought. Nay, I will not do that! Besides, say not that every trace of royalty has been taken from you. I trust that you have the royal jewel 'round your neck."

"I do—one secret treasure that a man may kill for," she said sadly.

"It is a great and evil thing to mistrust your servant so," he told her soberly. "I excuse your momentary fear, but you must not continue to accuse me to yourself. Too many storybooks have affected you."

Just then Reynald brought up the horse. The knight leading the horse looked out of place in his crown and ermine robe. "Ride for your lives," he murmured to Herron. "The gate is breaking down. You have only minutes to get a head start and escape."

"Aye. Come, majesty." Herron and the Princess led the horse out of the narrow hole in the wall. Reynald followed.

"Beloved Princess, farewell," he called after her.

"If I live to see my father, you and your treacherous wife shall be hanged," she called back to him.

"Nevertheless, farewell, sweet Princess," Reynald said. "These words have dropped to the ground between us. Think nothing of them when the time comes." And he shaded his eyes with his hands.

Herron lifted the Princess onto the saddle and swung up behind her.

"Remorse and shame shall drive those words back at you," he told her as he urged Javelin to a trot through the heavy trees. "This night Reynald will lay down his life for your majesty."

"He plans to claim the throne."

"Nay. You have no understanding. Now hush, I must listen."

The woods were dim with the settling night. In the distance, from the other side of the castle, they could hear horns blowing and horses screaming. But at that moment the battle was still small and intense, focused on the castle gates. The woods were safe yet.

Herron hurried his horse on. "Javelin's specially trained," he whispered. "He knows these woods by night, and so do I. That will give us a good lead."

For the first time, the Princess took some thought of the besieged castle and the people inside.

"I thought the battle would have to be halted when darkness fell."

"Nay. Above this canopy of branches, the moon and stars are out. Rigel has them and his torchbearers to guide his army. You must pity your subjects that fall into his hands."

"I won't pity Reynald."

"Oh sorrow, that my Princess should be so embittered. You seek revenge on your truest friend and spare no thought for your own people. It had been better for me to have fought and died by Reynald's side than to know how little the Princess counts the lives of her people. But I must deliver this miserable package to my King."

His rebuke stung her into resentful and hurt silence. They rode on without speaking.

For some time anger and confusion fought in the

Princess's heart, but at last these gave way to a stiffness in her limbs, then sleepiness. At last she dozed against him, falling into a deep sleep.

2
What Happened in the Fog

Herron pulled the horse up short, waking the young Princess.

"What—" she began.

"Shhhh." He turned, craning his neck, listening. For a moment Rosalynn thought she heard the faintest rattle of metal on metal, as might come from a horse's martingales or bit. For the first time she wondered what would happen if she fell into the hands of Rigel's soldiers. So far, they had seemed remote to her—an evil that only Reynald's soldiers had to deal with, always on the other side of the gates or across the wide river.

Now she felt curiously frail and unsafe with only the thin mist separating her from danger.

Herron urged the horse into a run. As he did, an arrow whizzed overhead. Herron pulled Javelin off the path and into the whipping branches of the forest. But Javelin knew where he was being driven. He quickly found a narrow deer trail and thundered down it as it wound along.

Herron, his cowl pulled low over his head, bent forward to shelter the Princess. For her part, she held on as bravely as she could and didn't scream or cry.

The woods were lighter now. Dawn was approaching. A morning fog hung thick amid the trunks of the trees.

At last he urged Javelin through a barricade of feathery pine saplings, and they emerged onto the main path again. And again, Herron fell silent and craned his head back, listening.

"We've doubled back," he began in a low voice. "We should be behind them—agh!"

She heard a terrible swish with his outcry and saw a feathered dart imbedded in the back of his shoulder.

"Go!" he cried, and kicked Javelin forward. "Face forward and stay low, Princess. I have to watch the path." And he urged Javelin harder until they were flying along.

But Herron was bleeding freely, and his left hand was weakening. The weakness would grow as he bled. He wouldn't be able to keep ahead of the pursuit.

"Rigel means to kill you," he told her. "We have only one hope—to decoy his men." They rounded a bend, and again Herron turned Javelin aside into the trees. Then he pulled to a silent halt behind a sturdy stand of pines and shrubbery. Through the fringe of branches they saw two riders thunder by, crossbows held before them.

"'Twas good for me it was a crossbow dart," he whispered. "An arrow from a longbow would have gone clean through me at that distance."

He looked down at her, and Rosalynn saw the drops of perspiration on his forehead and eyebrows, beading together and running down his lean, kind face.

A genuine pity struck her heart. "Oh, Herron," she began.

"You must escape," he said. "Slide down—on the right side, so I can help you."

He helped her slide down Javelin's muscular shoulder. Then he handed his small pack of bread and dried meat down to her.

"You must make for the river—down this deer trail—while they comb these woods," he whispered. "In a few days, your good father the King will pass this way. For my part, I will decoy those soldiers. As long as they think you're on my saddle they will chase me. Go quickly, Rosalynn." And he darted off again. In moments she heard the halloo of the enemy soldiers calling to each other. It was then that she realized that the forest was full of them.

She crept softly down the deer trail, eyes roving, back tingling, and waiting for another terrible dart out of the fog.

She began to be aware of something else—hoofbeats? marching boots? Then she realized it was the river rushing past. She hurried toward the sound and suddenly pitched right over the edge of the deer trail, hit the side of the steep bank, and toppled down to the water. At the bottom the bank sloped so that she stopped short from falling in, but her clothes were wet and muddy all over and torn in places. The bank had bruised her, and her pride was injured. More than anything, Rosalynn wanted her father or her nurse in that dreadful moment—even Reynald would have been welcome. She sighed, suddenly missing him as she inspected herself for scrapes and bruises. Was this what Herron had meant when he had predicted her remorse?

Then she looked around and caught sight of the precious bag of food, spinning down the river and slowly sinking beneath the current. It was hopelessly out of reach, then out of sight after a moment. Rosalynn pulled her knees up, buried her face into them, and cried.

These tears didn't last long. Young as she was, she knew that she couldn't be saved by sitting on the bank and crying. From up beyond the Bridge, the river flowed down past the King's castle in the north toward his brother's castle in the south. She could walk downriver to reach her uncle.

At first Rosalynn thought to do this and even set her foot forward to begin. Then she caught herself. She knew nothing of the land in the south, nothing of the people. She wasn't even sure how to get to her uncle's castle. And worse than that, the enemy soldiers were moving south, looking for her.

On the other hand, she could count on loyal farmers in the north to hide her. She knew the land up there much better and could stay hidden. Besides all these reasons, *home* was in the north. With the innocence of never having seen war before, she thought longingly of her nurse and all the knights who were her friends. She would return to them, war or no war, she told herself, and be welcomed by them.

So thinking, she set herself to the long task of walking up the river.

* * * *

Meanwhile, Rigel of Folger was inspecting what was left of the castle. In the courtyard, his men were trimming and cutting broad oak trees to make new gates. His corporals were hammering up rules of the new military occupation.

"It only remains," he said to Varger, his lieutenant, "to find that princess—Rosebush or whatever she is called—and make an end of her."

"I received word that the scouts saw one of Bracken's famous riders speeding south with a little maid," Varger said, grimacing unpleasantly. "I sent twenty men after them."

"Hmm. They must be fleeing to the Duke's castle. He's her uncle. Send more men down if you have to. Have a detail of them begin at the Duke's residence and sweep back toward us to cut them off. I'm determined to end their royal family."

"As you command, my Lord Rigel. Shall we bury the King?"

"Yes. But I want to lay eyes on him, first. It pays to be sure. And it pays to keep his crown and rings for myself. Lead on."

Varger led Rigel into the stone buildings of the living quarters, through empty and desolate hallways that echoed their boot steps, past burned and gutted rooms, up a marble stairway now chipped and stained, up to the King's quarters.

"Wait here," Rigel said as he entered. He pushed sideways through the doorway. In a moment he was back, and his huge fist sent Varger reeling across the ruined carpet of the hallway.

"You fool! That's not the King!" he bellowed.

"But—" Varger didn't have a chance to say any more as his master hurled him backwards again and sent him to the carpet. For the moment, Varger decided it would be wisest to stay there.

"He's escaped! Escaped! That's Reynald in there— dressed up as king!"

"Reynald?"

Varger was no small man, but Rigel swung him up by his tunic as though the lieutenant were a boy. "Reynald!" he roared. "King Bracken's advisor! He dressed as the King to fool us! Oh! Why did I leave it to you!" He threw Varger down and stamped down the hallway. "Bring me word! Bring me any knight or soldier left alive! Use force, use promises, use anything! But find out where the real king is, or there'll be *two* burials today!" And he stormed down the stairs.

* * * *

Hunger now troubled Rosalynn as she picked her way along the narrow bank. The waters were becoming stronger and deeper as she walked upriver, so that it was impossible to stay hidden by keeping to the river bottom. She had to walk up on the bank.

But the trees grew close, offering shelter from roving eyes. She only wished she might find some wild berries to eat. Her shoes were also troubling her. The wet, muddy leather made her feet raw and blistered her soles and the backs of her heels.

At last she stopped to rest in a grassy spot, pulling off her shoes and throwing herself down. So far, she had made good time, but it was certain she would have fallen asleep there in the grassy shade if hoofbeats hadn't roused her. She scurried on all fours into the undergrowth around the trees. Seconds later, two soldiers bearing the crest of Folger on their helmets burst out of the forest and sat looking at the powerful river.

"Too steep here," one said in disgust. "I don't fancy climbing down there to bring up a helmetful for this old nag." And he startled his horse by giving it a disgusted slap on the neck.

"Let's go down a mile. It slows down around that bend where the river widens so much. Come on."

And they wheeled their horses around, then galloped away.

Heart pounding, Rosalynn put her painful shoes back on and resumed her walk.

But the afternoon sun was merciless. Although she had as much water to drink as she wanted, she would have traded the whole river for a piece of bread and her comfortable walking shoes.

She had to stop often to rest, and it seemed that each time she stood up again, the cruel shoes rubbed all the scratches and blisters into fresh pain. For a while her hunger had seemed to subside on its own, but with late afternoon it came back, double strength.

At last she found a hollow in the ground, close to the shelter of the trees. She took one last drink from the river, untied her shoes and pulled them off, then curled up and fell asleep.

* * * *

"The lord's in a dither
He couldn't tell whither
His rabbits had fled.
An imposter's in bed
The crown upon his head
And Rosalynn, Rosalynn, Rosalynn's wed!"

The Jester sang and laughed wickedly. "Oh-ee" he squealed at Varger, showing almost toothless gums. "You're going to catch it from his lordship now!"

"Oh, give me peace," Varger growled over his plate. "And don't sing that silly song."

One of Rigel's captains looked up from their table where the group of them were eating. "Song's wrong anyway," he observed, wiping his mouth on the back of his hand. "The Princess ain't wed—not by a long shot."

"That's poetic license," the Jester told him airily, putting his stockinged feet up on the table. "Poetic license enables a man to say whatever he wishes, so long as it's in verse."

Varger's long arm shot out and toppled the Fool out of his chair. "Get your feet off the table! And see here—" he exclaimed, pointing a drumstick at the Jester who was rising in wrath from the floor. "See here; you may be Rigel's Fool, but if he catches you making fun of his poetry, he'll hang you up by your ears for target practice!"

It was sadly true that Rigel wrote the worst poetry ever heard. He believed a king should be very literate and educated. But since he wasn't, he only pretended to be. It was the one thing that even the Jester didn't dare joke about openly. But even the toughest captains and soldiers smirked when the Jester both imitated Rigel's poor poetry and pretended to defend it. Only Varger didn't think it was funny.

"Cool your temper, Friend and Master Varger," the Jester said, cooling his own as he stood up and took his chair. "The court Fool must make his jokes, as they say. I warrant you could use a dose of laughter right about now. His lordship's breathing down your neck about the King and the Princess, eh?"

"You attend to your foolery and your belly!" Varger said, standing up. "I will attend to my duties!"

He was about to stalk out when a messenger ran in. "Oh my master, Varger," he said. "Pardon my intrusion! The search parties flushed out a rider at dawn. They testify that he was carrying the Princess Rosalynn!"

"Yes? And?"

"They shot the rider and killed him, sir. But the Princess escaped. Somehow he set her down without their knowing it."

"Where is the body?" Varger asked.

The messenger looked startled. "The body, sir?"

"Of the rider! He may have been carrying orders to the King!"

"I—" The messenger turned white. "I don't know, sir."

"Well, how do you know he's dead?"

"He was shot out of the saddle, sir, by three different men. Of course we assumed—"

"You assumed? You—" Varger raised a heavy hand to strike him, then caught himself. "No. I will leave you to Rigel's fury. Let him have you executed if he so wills. Report to him, and tell him that I myself will lead a troop of men to find and search for the fallen rider! Begone!"

The terrified messenger raced out.

"How conveniently you will make yourself disappear from Rigel's wrath," the Fool observed. It was no surprise to anybody that the Jester knew of Varger's present disgrace before his lord. The Jester knew every detail of who was in favor and who wasn't.

Instead of becoming angry at the Jester's remark, Varger smiled wryly. "That's how I got where I am, Jester. Strategy." And he walked out.

The Jester gave a snort of laughter, but looking at his eyes, a person would know he hadn't forgotten Varger's push.

"Now what?" Rigel asked as the messenger entered Rigel's temporary throne room.

The carpenters had hurriedly created an imposing wooden throne for Rigel and had resurrected a scarred table on which he was signing legal notices to the captive people of Bracken.

Faint light came from sputtering candles. There were chinks here and there in the walls.

"My Lord Rigel," the messenger began, then fell on his knees and poured out his story. "Forgive your foolish scouts," he pleaded. "We are all new recruits sent out by our captain. We did not mean to fail you by deserting the rider's body. Even now Varger runs to reclaim the body and search it."

"Get up!" Rigel exclaimed, and the man rose quickly. "Ten strokes of the lash for each of you. You say south, eh? He must have been heading for the estate of the King's brother. I assume the King is with the Duke, then. Well, the battle will be more difficult and therefore more enjoyable, for the end is certain. Though the Duke's weak castle will fall to us, I enjoy a contest of the wills. We can execute them all together when we take them.

"As for that brat the Princess—she must be on foot south to join them. Tell the captains to send out more spies to comb the land for her and keep her from rejoining them. Meanwhile I will send over to Folger for the army to be massed and to come over the Bridge. Go."

"Yes, my lord."

"And report to the brig for the lash—you and your scouts. Mark me, boy, you'd better hope that rider died. I'll see that you never forget to check a fallen enemy again."

"Yes, my lord." The messenger bowed and hurried out. Ten lashes was a cruel punishment, but not nearly as cruel as what he had expected. Rigel was indeed pleased with his war. He expected the tiny land to be in his power very shortly.

* * * *

Morning came, but Rosalynn missed the glorious dawn. She slept through the rising of the birds and through the steady ringing of the stonecutters upriver. It was hunger that finally roused her. She looked around, confused for a moment, then remembered all that had passed.

As soon as she sat up, her whole body rebelled. It was stiff and sore and enraged with hunger. She could not put on her shoes at all. The swollen feet had become way too big, and they were too painful to be forced.

For the first time Rosalynn began to understand how grim her situation was. Perhaps not surprisingly, she thought first of Reynald, who had always been her protector. She sat in the hollow, sheltered by the tree, and cried, wishing he would come and take her back to the castle where it was safe. And then she thought of Herron, riding away with a feathered shaft in his shoulder and the enemy behind him. Was he dead now, or imprisoned?

She cried for a long time, but at last she made herself stand up. A wave of faintness washed over her, and she caught hold of the tree for support. It was in doing this that she saw the cottage.

For a moment it swam in front of her eyes, but then she focused on it. It was indeed a cottage. A stonecutter's cottage!

3
Enemy Territory

Limping on her aching feet, Rosalynn made her way through the prickly undergrowth toward the log house. An inviting wisp of smoke curled from the chimney. That one sign of cheer and rest and food drove away the rest of her caution. She did not bother to notice how dirty and stained the shutters were, how unkept the plot of ground. The garden—what there was—was choked with weeds. The front door, a scarred and chipped leftover from another house, hung by straps instead of pegs, as though it had hurriedly been put up and then left in that slipshod state.

She noticed none of these things—only the wisp of smoke that gave her hope. So she picked her way over the rough and prickly ground and at last knocked on the scarred, ugly door.

It was pulled open by a slope-shouldered woman, not ugly but untidy indeed, who scratched herself and gaped at Rosalynn.

"What are you doing here—what with war ravaging so close? Get you home! I can't be 'sponsible for you, y'hear? Go on, now!"

"Wait!" Rosalynn pushed against the closing door. "I am Princess Rosalynn! By my father's name and crown, I beg you to help me!" And she grasped the woman's untidy skirts. The woman, who had been turning away, turned back and stared down at her.

"Why—why so it is! Sure and I've seen you that often in the parades! Come inside." And she pulled the princess into the dirty cabin.

Rosalynn tried to explain her situation, saying, "I've been walking since yesterday morning. They've shot my friend and protector, Herron the Rider, and—and—" For the second time that morning, she burst into tears. Now that she was back with human companionship, her sorrows and fears rushed on her more keenly.

But the woman did no more than gape at her, and Rosalynn stopped. "Please, could I have something to eat?" she asked when she controlled herself.

"Yes, yes, of course," the woman said, and scurried over the dirt floor to her hearth. She hadn't invited Rosalynn to sit down, but Rosalynn did so anyway, too footsore to stay standing.

A light began to come into the woman's eyes as she stirred up what was left of the morning's porridge. She had read the notices posted here and there along the paths. A price was on Rosalynn's head—one hundred gold pieces for the return of the Princess.

Of course, in peace time the woman never would have dared to bring the Princess—nor any other citizen— of Bracken to harm. But she was only as good as the laws of the land, no better. Rigel made the laws now— he had been making quite a few even since taking over two days ago. Now it was *legal* to sell the Princess for reward, and so it would be all right, or at least not wrong, in the peasant woman's eyes.

When she spoke, she spoke softly. "All I have is toast and porridge just now. But my man will be home at midday with meat he's traded for. You can breakfast now, and sleep until he comes."

"Yes, thank you," Rosalynn said. She hoped the woman would keep her. "I can work for you in exchange."

"Now, now!" the woman exclaimed, genuinely surprised. "Whoever heard of a princess working for a peasant!"

Rosalynn blinked, surprised in her turn. For herself, she had never heard of a guest not doing *something* to make his own company pleasant, whether it was lending help or simply supplying conversation. She had visited Reynald's quarters enough to know this.

At last Rosalynn's eyes touched all points of the dirty cabin, and her mind grasped the woman's ignorance of manners and lack of courtesy. But she supposed it all came from being uneducated. She pushed back her uneasiness.

The woman set food before her, and the Princess ate ravenously of the porridge and thin toast. For a few moments she almost forgot her own manners.

Even before she was finished, her eyes began to feel heavy, and they felt heavier and heavier now that her painfully empty stomach had been filled. But now the woman spoke to her. "How ever did you escape the battle, what with your father the King slain and all?"

"My father isn't dead," she said, surprised. "He is at my uncle's residence this very moment. And I know he will drive out this pretender, Rigel."

"Not dead! Why the very man is to be buried this morning!" the woman exclaimed, staring at her. "He died wearing his crown and winter robe."

"That wasn't my father!" she retorted, disgust and leftover anger rising in her eyes. "'Twas Reynald—" Then she caught herself. Her blue eyes rose from the bowl in shock and dismay. "Did you say he was dead?"

But the woman had a shrewd light in her eye. "How cunning! Your father dresses him up as king, then gets away free, with enough time to plan a counter-attack! Hmph! There's royalty for you!"

Rosalynn didn't answer, not noticing the insult to her father and to royalty.

Suddenly, her heart grasped Reynald's plan to save the King and to save her. He had offered himself to give the riders time to warn the true king. And in killing what he thought was the King, Rigel had stopped the sweep of his troops from destroying the whole land.

She felt her jaw twitch. Her mind went numb. For a moment she sat as though an arrow had suddenly pierced her heart. Indeed, one had—an arrow of remorse and guilt.

The woman was still prattling on, "Wonder of wonders," she was saying. "Of all the things that go on at court—who'd a' thought it?"

Then she saw Rosalynn's bowed head and said briskly, "Come now, you'll be wanting to sleep."

She led the Princess into the back room, where heavy shutters across the window hid the squalor inside. In the gloom Rosalynn made out a bed with a straw mattress.

"Lie down here. I'll wake you in time for a good dinner, my Princess."

Rosalynn obeyed, still numb. Yet, though her mind was confused and her heart sorely grieved, she was too exhausted to weep yet. Instead of brooding and crying, she fell into a deep sleep, unconscious even of the pain in her feet, which the woman had neglected.

A couple of quiet hours passed, but she woke up when the front door of the cottage was dragged open and then slammed.

Instantly two voices rose at once in excitement, the peasant woman sharing her news with her husband. Rosalynn stirred.

"Aye," he was saying in his slow, ponderous way. "There be soldiers a-plenty from here to the castle. Like as not we could hail a couple—"

"What? And be cheated by them? No, we'll bind her hand and foot; you must borrow a donkey—"

"With what excuse—"

"Shh! Keep your voice down. She's exhausted, but she may awaken."

Rosalynn by instinct closed her eyes and kept still. The door to the back room opened a crack, then closed as softly as the leather straps would permit.

"Sleeping soundly. All that walking on her royal feet did her in."

"I'll go see about that donkey before dinner."

The front door opened and then slammed again. For a moment Rosalynn lay trembling. But then she forced herself to move, knowing that they meant to surrender her up as soon as possible. She left the bed without a rustle and went to the shutters.

Some light seeped in through the chinks between the logs, enabling her to see in the gloom. Using the same chinks as toeholds, she scrambled up and unlatched the shutter. Tree climbing had never been approved as a royal pastime, but she had done it before, and it served her now.

She climbed the rough inside wall, straddled the sill for a moment while she brought her other leg up, then dropped down for a painful landing.

Her ankles gave way under her weight, and she struggled not to cry out from the pain in her feet. After a moment the enraged pain subsided to its steady throbbing.

Her shoes, unusable as they were, had been left in the front room. There was no getting them now. Without a backward glance, she plunged into the brush, limping and jogging for the river.

For some minutes she jogged along as quickly as she could, certain that they would be pursuing her any moment.

She came to the river and would have despaired of outdistancing them but for two otters that she startled on the bank. They jumped and slid down the bank, disappearing without a splash or ripple in the water, as though they had crawled *into* the bank instead. She fell on hands and knees and peered down.

At this point in the river, the trees grew right up to the bank, but the bank itself was high, with a five-foot overhang that jutted over the water below. The otters, she realized, had escaped *under* the bank.

Rosalynn's desire to hide overcame her fear of falling into the waters. Clinging to exposed roots here and there, she eased herself down the otters' slide. It curved under the overhang in the bank. Years of spring flooding had worn the bank away from beneath, exposing the tree roots and making a rough tunnel among them, a passageway to safety along the river.

She certainly couldn't stand up straight in the tunnel—there were places where she wondered at getting through at all. But other places were neatly hollowed out. She scurried along, sometimes crawling and climbing, sometimes running bent over with the cool and delicious earth beneath her tortured feet. The tree roots hung like vines over her in some places or tried to bar the way like fallen logs in other places.

Here and there she ran through oozing mud, and this eased her sore feet, too. Her heart grew a little lighter. Hunger had been filled, at least, and her pain somewhat eased by the mud. And now the tree roots were less thick and less numerous. She had escaped danger again.

But then her heart darkened. Reynald, truest friend to the crown, she had scorned and threatened. And the stonecutter's wife, treacherous and deceitful, she had trusted. Guilt pierced her heart again. She had deserved to die, she thought, worth nothing better than the wife's trickery after her treatment of Reynald.

Again, keen loneliness and fear cut her like a knife. Images of her nurse, the kennel man, the stable boys who played horse with her, these all rose like phantoms in her mind. Where were they? Any one of them, she knew, would shelter her at any risk. But they were most likely dead or imprisoned.

Hoofbeats from on top of the bank brought her to a halt. She waited, and the hoofbeats stopped.

"Vanished completely, little fox!" a deep voice boomed.

"Rigel is out hunting her now," a second added.

"That sniveling stonecutter's wife said she'd likely gone this way. Where could the brat be hiding? Are you sure you don't see her down the river there?"

"Not a speck," the second answered. "She's not along the river, that's for sure. Unless she had wings, she couldn't have gone farther than this in bare feet."

"I knew all along she'd head south," the first voice said. "She's making for her father."

"Well, that's not what his lordship says."

"Oh, aye! I wish he didn't have the Fool riding with him. Hateful fellow. I never turn my back to that Jester." And the deep voice added a snort of disgust.

"Nor I," the second voice answered. "And I pity the brat if they get hold of her. I know it is treasonous to pity her, but in truth, she would do better with a merciful fast sword from me than the execution that the Fool would cook up for her!"

There was a pause, and then the first said, somewhat gruff with guilt and emotion, "Aye. I don't pity her— I mean, I would do my duty by my Lord Rigel, but it puts me in a sweat to think of it, man. Give me an enemy with a sword in his fist, and I'll deal with him. But a child—still, as you say, better from us than from the Fool. Come on."

She heard them wheel their horses around and gallop off. After a breathless moment of listening, she moved on.

The day had been cloudy. and in the late afternoon a steady rain began falling. Rosalynn's passageway became slick, then dangerous. She crawled on hands and knees, perilously close to sliding into the river, catching onto whatever roots she could find in the tunnel that had become sparse and bare. It was little more than a narrow shelf here, and she could not climb the overhanging bank to get to the top.

There was nothing to do but inch her way forward, while lightning flashed over the waters and thunder rolled. Her arms trembled, whether from cold or fever or weariness, she didn't know. She made herself think only of moving ahead, searching for rough places in the mud where her hands would not slip.

This worked for a while, but she was startled to feel a coolness rush over her bare feet. She looked back. A swell of water had rushed into the tunnel behind her and then out again. The river was moving faster—was it rising, too?

"It's only waves," she told herself, "not a flood."

She didn't know if a river could flood so quickly. But even if somebody had told her that it could—and in fact was—it would have done her no good. There was no way out but forward.

More waves lapped into the passageway, and then suddenly one great swell rushed over her, choking and blinding her for a moment. The mud beneath her turned to silt, and she toppled into the river.

But Rosalynn's flailing hand caught a root thrust up from the eroded bank, and she held on while cold water rushed over her. She got her head clear and looked up. For a moment, astonishment and awe replaced her fear of drowning.

Enormous oak pillars were thrust up out of the river. They were set in stone-and-mortar sockets, each socket the width and height of a castle tower.

Still clutching the root, she craned her neck to look up higher. The Bridge was before her, standing over her like a giant's fence or like a company of stone-and-oak sentinels on the river.

4
The Bridge and Beyond

The cypress root held.

She climbed it hand over hand, as she would have climbed a rope, pulling herself back into the disintegrating passageway. The bottom was awash with silt and water, but she had to go on.

Rosalynn crawled flat on her stomach, mercifully held fast by the sucking mud beneath the loose mud on top, but washed now and then by numbing waves that swept over her.

The pillars of the Bridge were making the waters swirl and sweep over her, but the Bridge also meant a landing of some sort. She crawled a little farther and felt gravel beneath her. The rain suddenly stopped pelting her in the shelter under the Bridge, and she scrambled up a shelving embankment.

She was under the ramp of the Bridge, sheltered for a moment under a roof as high as a castle ceiling. Panting and exhausted, she looked around. The rain still beat down around the ramp, and the water swirled below.

But a new cunning—born from danger—told her what to do. Soldiers lined the river and filled the forest. She had only one place to go, one place where surely no one would look for her—over the Bridge and into Folger.

No one among the peasantry there would recognize her, surely. And it would take only a moment to fling her jewel of royalty away forever.

Cautiously, she climbed up the steep embankment, higher and higher, staying under cover of the ramp that slanted down to earth above her. The ground began to level as the ramp met the road. When there was only a crawlspace left under the ramp, she peeped out into the pouring rain.

Anybody guarding the Bridge was along the path ahead, probably huddled into a cloak and feeling gloomy. She saw nobody.

Rosalynn climbed onto the ramp. How high the Bridge was, strong enough to enable an army to pass over with row on row of iron-shod horses and armored soldiers! Her bare feet padded up the long and broad ramp, higher and higher, while the rain lashed down and lightning flashed. Still higher and higher she ran, up the smooth and sloping ramp, as high as a battlement. The trees on either side disappeared. Winds thrashed the Bridge, humming through the suspension cables. The river below was a mere stream from this height, and she didn't look down a second time.

Twin pillars soared above her, upholding the suspension cables on either side of her. These cables were as thick as logs, and from them the suspension ropes that held up the flooring of the Bridge were secured.

She hurried on, buffeted by the winds and rain. She raced past more pillars—many more, for the Bridge spanned a full mile over the river.

Then she was on the ramp on the other side, and it was there that the soldiers, changing their watch, saw her.

Even in the storm she heard their shouts and the blare of a trumpet. She leaped off the ramp and into the underbrush—a drop of five feet now that she was so close to the end. It knocked the wind out of her, but she was up and running instantly, through the thickest brambles and thickets she could find, crawling here on all fours, running there, straining and listening in some places. She thought she should fling the jewel away and persuade them if they caught her that she was only a frightened peasant.

But when her fingers touched the jewel, she thought of Reynald, and suddenly to renounce her throne was disgraceful, as disgraceful as her rebuke to him had been. Her fingers dropped from the jewel, and she left it alone.

The soldiers were on horseback, forcing their way through with difficulty. She went on, but now, suddenly, she felt every motion of her exhausted body. In two days she had pushed herself beyond what few of the sturdiest children could have endured, for she had been spurred by terror. But now her feet refused to run as fast. The undergrowth seemed to resist her even more when she tried to force her way through.

She thought for a moment that she'd lost them, and she sank down full length on the ground. But suddenly there was a hacking behind her, as somebody chopped his way with a sword through the dense brush that was hiding her.

She gasped, crawled forward behind a stand of trees, and collapsed again, tensely waiting. Then she had a sense of somebody close by, and she looked around. Her eyes scanned back and forth, and she noticed the tree in front of her—how its gray bark fell down its trunk in soft, cloth-like folds. It was not bark, but real cloth—the cloth of a gray cloak, right in front of her face. She had crawled to the feet of her enemy.

Rosalynn looked no higher than the hem of the cloak. Exhaustion and fear met; her heart gave out, and she buried her face into her arm and sobbed.

"Herron!" she cried, and was still.

Then for a long time she knew nothing—not thunder, not lightning, not even pain. Only blackness and silence.

But at last a light seeped in—firelight. And something was tickling at her sore feet, soothing and softening the scarred skin and bruised toes. She opened her eyes and breathed in a pungent smell like strong mint. She saw a fireplace, a bench, a spinning wheel. And for a long moment she lay without thought, staring blankly at this homely picture before her. Then the tickling on her feet began again—only it was more of a steady, regular, and pleasant feeling than tickling. It eased the fires burning across her heels and insteps and up her shins.

Rosalynn's eyes looked down to her feet and saw a woman carefully bathing them, rinsing them again and again over a basin full of water mixed with something else. Rosalynn's feet looked terrible—swollen and bruised and out of shape.

"This should ease the pain while it helps heal them," the woman said. She had steeped a cloth in the pungent liquid, and now she wrapped this cloth over one injured foot, wrapping it loosely and setting it gently on the sheet.

The gentle action and quiet voice brought tears to the eyes of the Princess as she watched. The woman used another cloth for the Princess's other foot. When she finished, she looked up and saw the two tears. "You had a narrow escape," she said kindly. "But the soldiers went pelting past us as I held you inside my cloak. Their eyes were not sharp, and they took us for a part of the trees."

"She held me inside her cloak," Rosalynn thought, as though she had to interpret the words again to herself. The woman took the basin away and came back. She sat on the edge of the bed.

"I burned your clothes," she said. "Rigel sent out notices with your description printed and a reward offered. Your clothes would have given you away, ruined as they were. I can cobble up something for you—make you appear a proper maid." She smiled and touched the Princess's hair.

"You know who I am, then?" Rosalynn whispered.

She nodded. "The Princess Rosalynn." And then her fingers reverently touched the jewel that hung around Rosalynn's neck. "This, if nothing else, made you known to me."

"And this is Folger?"

"Of course it is."

The Princess studied the woman's eyes, which were that hazel blue so often called gray. She swallowed and asked, "Aren't you going to give me up to Rigel?"

The smile became tender. "No, dear Princess. Nothing would make me surrender a child to the executioner's block. And besides, I am not of this land, but serve a king in the north. Rigel suffers my presence here because I know medicine."

Then she stood up, went to the hearth, and ladled out a steaming bowl from a pot hanging by the fire.

"This is strong broth, perhaps disagreeable," she said, carrying it back. "But I worry for your lungs and chest. You were freezing cold and soaking wet when I carried you back here. Only a strong cure will keep you from a serious illness. Taste this." And she offered a spoonful of the soup to Rosalynn, ready to coax the Princess.

But Rosalynn willingly took spoonful after spoonful of it, until the bowl was empty.

"Well," the woman said. "It *would* have been more difficult if you hadn't been half starved. It should strengthen your lungs."

"Thank you," Rosalynn said. She saw that though the woman's face was young, her rich, thick hair—hanging in a coil at the back of her neck—had wisps of gray in it here and there. Yet she moved as one in great youth, and her voice was the voice of a young woman.

The woman took the bowl away and straightened the bedding for Rosalynn, who took this as a signal that she should lie down again and obeyed it. "You must not worry or be afraid," the woman said kindly, smoothing the girl's forehead with a cool hand. "For now, think only that you're safe at last."

As the woman lifted the sheets and comforters to straighten them, Rosalynn saw her own condition better. She was wearing a tunic as a nightgown. Below the hem, her knees were bandaged, and she caught a glimpse of sores and scabs on her shins. She felt a mustard plaster on her chest. Her hands, stiff and bruised, were uncovered. And her hair had been cut, washed, and carefully dried to keep her from becoming chilled again.

The blankets were heavy and soft, and they smelled delicious—like flowers in a garden. She did feel safe, and no bed in her father's castle was so comfortable.

As she fell asleep, she looked at the woman and tried to muster the strength to say thank you—to ask who she was and to say something courteous.

"Sleep," the woman said, laughing and kissing her forehead. "Sleep, Princess."

And Rosalynn slept.

For ten long hours she didn't move, didn't stir at all while the woman sat nearby, hemming up a dress to fit the girl. Then at last she rolled over a little, mumbled something, and slept on, entering into the gates of a normal sleep that showed she was well. Six hours later, she stretched, winced, and woke up with a start.

"Oh, me," she exclaimed as every muscle prickled in rebellion.

"Ah, you're stiff and sore yet," the woman agreed. "And you feel it, now that you've rested. Eat this oatmeal and milk, and then I'll attend to your feet."

Rosalynn ate every bit of the breakfast—though it was closer to supper time—but she was so hungry she hardly tasted it. She watched anxiously as the woman pounded together some herbs and mixed them in a pan of boiling hot water. She set in two more cloths to steep, then poured some boiling water together with cool water into another basin and brought this to Rosalynn's bed.

The woman unwrapped the Princess's feet. "Somewhat better," she said cheerfully, though Rosalynn couldn't see much difference. "They may look bad, but they'll not hurt so much anymore. The poultice drew out the infection." And she rinsed them again and again, one at a time. Then she wrapped them again in the steeped cloths.

After she had put her things away, she sat by Rosalynn and gathered the Princess's hands into her lap. "Now we must plan, Princess. Your father the King will be ready to war soon, and maybe Rigel will be diverted from his search for you. As soon as your feet heal, we must find our way to your father."

"First," Rosalynn said, "do you know of my father's castle? Were many killed?"

The woman's gaze became gentler still, and Rosalynn knew the battle had been tragic.

"Dear Princess," the woman said. "Many indeed were lost. All the captains died at war or were executed. And one man who posed as king was killed. All the royal staff and attendants have been imprisoned or executed."

Rosalynn's eyes lowered. "The man who posed as king—" she began. "Reynald—"

"He saved the kingdom," the woman told her. "For when Rigel thought the King had fallen, he spared the land. Otherwise, he would have swept in harder, more cruelly, and taken your uncle's castle in the south as well. But for twelve hours he was fooled, and in those twelve hours, word of the attack reached your father, and he was able to prepare his defenses. Even now the people are flocking to him to join the fight and save the land."

"I wronged Reynald when I left," she said, and before the steady eyes of the woman, Rosalynn was even more ashamed. Under that honest and steady gaze she realized that she should have believed in Reynald, should have submitted to his plans in the knowledge that he was wiser than she and faithful. Now she understood that her own pride had made her distrust him. She dropped her eyes. "I accused him wrongfully. I hated him, and all that time he was preparing to die for me and the kingdom."

The woman could only look grave and sorrowful, and Rosalynn began to cry. "What have I done? He was my friend!" And she wept under a weight of guilt she had never felt before.

At last the woman pulled her close and said, "Surely a friend like that forgave you." But there was nothing she could say that made Rosalynn's crime any less a crime. It had been a horrible thing to hate Reynald.

"Now my people are imprisoned," Rosalynn mourned. "Why did Herron and Reynald save me? I deserved to die, not them!" She wept again while the woman held her, then looked up as an idea struck her. "If I went back to Rigel myself, do you think he would let the others go?" she asked.

"No!" the woman exclaimed. "You must never fall into his hands!" And she held the Princess more tightly. "You don't know his cruelties nor the scope of his plans," she said. Then she added, "So long as the royal line lasts, Rigel can never rest in his power in Bracken. So you must stay free."

She stroked the girl's hair. "Living for yourself is too miserable. Now you know that. You must live for your people instead, and as for yourself, you must believe that your friend Reynald forgave you. Wrong cannot be undone, but it can be forgiven."

Rosalynn nodded in agreement. Then, very clearly in her mind, she saw Reynald again, standing framed in the hole in the castle wall.

"These words of yours have dropped to the ground between us. Think nothing of them when the time comes."

She gave a little jump at the memory.

"What is it?" the woman asked.

"Oh, he did forgive me! Now I know what he meant!" she exclaimed. "He foresaw my sorrow." She was quiet a moment, but she added softly, "Oh, Reynald! If I could only see you once more." Then she was still. She looked up at the woman.

"We must carry out his plans," the woman said. She gently helped Rosalynn lie back down in the bed. "As soon as I know that you've recovered, I will lay plans to get you back to your father. He must still be quartered with the Duke, preparing a defense of the land."

Rosalynn nodded. The woman looked away and softly sang to herself:

"Come war, the soldier earns his trade
Beat the drums; my heart inspire.
Bring me my iron blade,
My helmet rivet on.
Bring me the prancing horse.
Gird on my sword of fire.

Nay, come there many boots
On cobblestones that ring?
Disarm me where the waters course.
My iron helm unhinge.
A riverboat shall be my horse.
One axe shall overthrow a king."

"Stay!" Rosalynn exclaimed, sitting up. "You must not sing that song!"

The woman smiled. "Why not?"

"It is the song of the castle guard!" Rosalynn told her. "The penalty for any common person singing that song in Bracken is death! The song must be closely guarded. It is not for the common people to sing."

"We are not in Bracken," the woman replied. "And I think the secret has been too closely guarded. Did your friend Reynald know this song?"

"Aye. Reynald taught it to me in the presence of my father and the captains."

"And did he not explain it to you?"

"Explain what?"

"The reason it was important."

"It is important because it is the mark of the castle guard or royalty. Like a password. In Bracken you would be taken for a spy if you sang it."

She shook her head. "The song is known outside of Bracken, Princess. It is known to anybody who will ponder over the lore of that ancient and tiny land. Your people and my people are distantly related. It was the architects of my country who came and built the Bridge as a favor to Bracken."

"Unhappy favor!" Rosalynn exclaimed. "They meant it for kindness, but it has undone us!"

"Nay, they made a safeguard. Enough of that for now. We must get to safety first."

Rosalynn settled back into the bed. But she began to feel uneasy in herself for having so quickly called the woman a common person and for having rebuked her. Reynald himself had warned her against rebuking others so quickly.

She felt the eyes of the woman on her, and she wondered if, after all, she had been wise to be so lordly with someone who held her life in her hand.

"Why help me?" the Princess asked at last, breaking her own uneasy silence. "There were those of my own people who would have betrayed me."

The woman didn't answer, not with words in the way a person would expect, but she fixed her eyes on Rosalynn's, and Rosalynn saw there a gentleness and kindness so deep that she was ashamed of herself for all she had thought and said in the last few moments.

"Pardon my haughty spirit," Rosalynn asked after a moment, lowering her eyes. "I am more arrogant than I can understand, even now. Whatever you choose to sing or say or order or decide, that I will abide by and obey." But there was no getting away from those eyes gazing down on her—eyes that had known, as keenly as Reynald had known, Rosalynn's arrogance and mistrust.

"Your decision pleases me. I forgive you. Close your eyes, little Princess."

And she put her hand over Rosalynn's eyes to shut them off from her own and relieve the Princess's embarrassment. In a moment the Princess fell asleep.

When morning came, Rosalynn ventured to walk a little, from bed to fireplace on the smooth wood floor. The muscle-pinching weariness and stiffness from the day before were eased a little now, thanks to a rubdown from the woman and some horrible-smelling liniment.

After helping to stem and sort herbs, she ate lunch, and then after a rest walked around the room, surveying the wonders that belonged to the wise woman—for so Rosalynn thought of her and called her.

There was a small well built by the hearth—not for drinking but for bathing. A mirror, small enough to be held in the hand, hung on one of the walls, close by the well. A clock stood in the corner opposite the mirror and well.

Cabinets and cupboards and drawers lined half the room. These, Rosalynn guessed, held different medicines and planting tools. A door in another corner led to the woman's bedroom. Pots, crochans, knives, and other utensils lined the wall by the hearth, across from Rosalynn's bed. All in all, the room was cozy and perfectly arranged. Rosalynn felt that in her own palace there was no room quite so cheerful and snug.

"I've finished your dress, Princess," the woman said. "Come and bathe."

After a cold dip in the well and a good wash, Rosalynn put on the garments the woman had made her. "The peasant clothing of Folger differs from ours," Rosalynn said, slipping on a clean tunic and then a knee-length dress of soft material. The dress had generous fullness to it; yet it was lightweight.

"These are the garments of a scholar," the woman said, adding, "a scholar out of my homeland. We will be regarded as foreigners, you and I, and so we are. But the Folgerians will hesitate before accosting two people of high rank from another land." She surveyed Rosalynn and nodded, satisfied. "I must make you some moccasins—soft and sturdy ones, and a traveling cloak, too. By the time I've done that, you should be ready to travel again."

"How will we go?" Rosalynn asked. "Shall we try to cross the Bridge at night?"

"Oh, no, Princess. It would be death to venture near it by land. We have to go downriver—south on this side for a long journey. I can show you."

She went to one of her cupboards and took out a scroll of paper. A map had been printed on it.

"The *X* in the circle marks this cottage," she told Rosalynn. "Here, on the right side. We must travel south on this side, through the cover of the forests, until we come to Herrington, a fishing village several days away. When we get there, we can skiff across the river and then make a run to the castle of the Duke of Small. If all goes well, the southern half of your kingdom will still be free a week from now, and we can walk there. But first we must get past the soldiers on this side, through the forest, and across the river." She looked pensive.

"Is it hopeless?" Rosalynn asked. "Are there that many dangers?"

"No, not hopeless, but yes, many dangers. It will be unpleasant at times. But I understand the forest fairly well. And you have a stout heart. We will need both knowledge and courage for what lies ahead."

Rosalynn felt warm from her word of praise. "I left Reynald behind, and I left Herron behind," she confessed. "But I promise, Woman, I won't leave you behind, even if it means capture and death from Rigel."

"Thank you," the woman said, and when the gentle and kind eyes fell on Rosalynn's eyes, Rosalynn knew for herself that she had promised a true promise. She met the gaze and in that moment wouldn't have traded their dangers and the coming journey together for anything.

5
The Fool Meets the Woman

They set out one fine morning. The woman had their bedroll and a small pack of food rolled together over her shoulder. Rosalynn had nothing to carry, though she had offered to help.

"No, but thank you," the woman said. "Should trouble meet us, I want you to be free to hide or run."

Rosalynn was glad to have her hands free. Being captured seemed unlikely on that fresh and dewy morning. Fresh smells were rising from the ground with the mist. Sunlight filtered through the trees and shone like diamonds on the glittering grass. Rising birds called to each other, and the pounding of the stonecutters came ringing over the waters from upriver.

"What a beautiful morning!" Rosalynn danced up the path and came back, taking the woman's free hand and swinging it.

"For a while you may prance," the woman said. "But after we come to the river path we have to stay quiet. Soldiers may be about."

Rosalynn nodded, too happy in the glorious morning to be afraid. At last her feet were better, encased now in soft leather moccasins. The woman had made the footwear herself, working night after night, greasing them and pounding fat into them to make them soft. After they had finally been as stretched and greased and pounded as possible, she had hammered an awl into them, making one careful hole at a time to sew the sinew through. Now Rosalynn wore the new shoes, softer and more comfortable than any pair she had ever owned before, and more sturdy than the heavy peasant shoes she had worn.

She stayed by the woman's side and looked at the surrounding trees as they plunged deeper into the forest. Then the woman looked down at her and smiled.

* * * *

The Fool struggled in the saddle and groaned. He shot a look of reproach at Rigel.

"A fine thing for a fool," he said. "Being blistered in the saddle! I cannot make foolery in pain like this!"

"Stop your whining!" Rigel said, while Varger, for the first time in days, grinned. The four other soldiers following the retinue took their cue from Varger and smiled among themselves.

"What good is a fool on a manhunt or scouting expedition?" he continued bitterly. "My place is at court, not here!"

"This is my court," Rigel said. "My forest, my lands."

His eyes surveyed the forest. They were riding on the Folger side of the river, inspecting the outlying patrols.

"That miserable brat escaped over here somewhere," Rigel muttered to Varger. "If we didn't have a war to fight, I could make a proper search for her."

"Don't worry, Lord Rigel," Varger said. "It will be a few days, and then the King of Bracken will fall. Then we can search for the girl at our leisure."

The Jester shifted again. "Miserable wench!" he exclaimed. "She'll pay dearly for my suffering this day! An hour on her part for every minute on mine."

"Hold your tongue," Varger growled. "We're soldiers, not cutthroats. She must die, but not by torture."

Rigel looked curiously at Varger.

The Jester scowled but changed the subject. "Where are we, my lord?" he asked. "To save my life, I have no sense of direction."

"A half mile east of the river and a mile south of the Bridge," Rigel said. "There's a cabin somewhere along here—I want to find it."

"A cabin, sire?" Varger asked. "Here?"

"Aye. The Bridge guards have stumbled onto it now and then and been helped by some woman there."

Varger cocked his head. "A woman? Getting a living from this worthless ground?"

"A foreigner," Rigel said. "Of a kingdom too great to make war against. I have tolerated her presence and made use of her medical skill, for she is a learned woman." He reined in. "The path divides down that way. You and the Fool make a search for some sign of smoke or a well. We will finish the inspection and then search the riverbank for footprints. Meet at the Bridge at high noon."

"As you wish, Lord Rigel." Varger bowed his head in obedience.

"And Varger—"

"Aye, Lord?"

"See if you and the Fool can manage to keep from blows, eh?"

"Of course." But there was no hint of a smile in Varger's face.

* * * *

The sun waxed full and golden in a hazy blue sky. Early summer heat beat down. The river shimmered in the glare. On the Bridge, tar bubbled between the planks.

But in the shade of the giant oak trees, the earth still felt cool and damp. The woman dug out a moist hollow for Rosalynn's tired feet and spread loose earth over her toes. The moccasins she set aside in the shade. She and Rosalynn ate fruit, both dried and fresh, and also some bread.

"The heat will oppress us if we journey now," the woman said, looking out at the sparkling wide river that shimmered in patches between the massive tree trunks. "We can sleep now and continue the journey in the cool evening."

She walked back into the brush where the foliage was thick and quickly went to work. In a few minutes she had hollowed out the inside of a thicket and strewn the bottom with boughs and leaves.

"Come here, Princess."

Carrying her moccasins, Rosalynn entered the thicket with her. The woman hastily wove some of the boughs together and took off her cloak in the narrow space, revealing a soft traveling gown underneath that was a larger version of Rosalynn's.

Rosalynn thought the thicket might be cramped and hot, but with the cool earth beneath and the shade covering them, they were comfortable. The woman covered her with the cloak to keep insects away.

"I will watch awhile," she said. "Sleep a little." And Rosalynn snuggled into the safe soft cloak and went to sleep.

* * * *

Varger and the Fool rode several miles south under the glaring sun, then wheeled back around to make a sweep through the forest.

"You take that path," Varger growled. "Even you couldn't get lost on it. It will lead you back up to the Bridge. I will search the bank area."

The Jester snorted and looked sly. "You're a trickster, Varger. Sure you aren't lying about this path?" He meant to sound sly and cunning, but Varger saw through it to his fear of being left in the woods.

"If I'd thought about it, I would have lied to lose you here," he said. "And counted it a favor to Rigel. But no. The path goes to the Bridge. Now get a move on!"

With head low and eyes slit, the Fool clumsily urged his horse up the trail. Varger galloped away.

Left to himself, the Fool grumbled and complained, but since no one was there to hear him, he quieted at last.

The heat of the day increased. He became more and more hungry. Suddenly he noticed with a little jump that the sun was directly overhead but that the Bridge was nowhere in sight. Even the sounds of the river were silent to him.

"That Varger!"

But nobody heard his accusation. He didn't have the sense to realize that he and Varger had ridden south together much more quickly than he was riding north.

He merely supposed that Varger had tricked him after all.

"I'll show that treacherous knave," he stormed, and brought his horse around again to retrace his way.

* * * *

Rosalynn yawned, stretched, and pushed the light cloak off her face. "Is it night yet?"

"Not quite, not even suppertime yet," the woman told her, watching through the leaves and stroking Rosalynn's hair. "The men in the fields will still be working. But you may put your moccasins on. The sun at least is well past its zenith."

Rosalynn sat up and put on her moccasins. The woman was listening and watching, and so the Princess waited until she was satisfied that all was safe.

They left the thicket, and the woman stirred it up inside and spread around the branches she had cleared. Then they walked on through the trees, in and out of sight of the glimmering river.

It was just twilight, and the bullfrogs beginning, when a weary and dirty Fool returned on his horse to the place where he had last seen Varger.

"Oh, that scoundrel!" he howled. "How could he dare? Rigel's own Fool—to suffer so! On you! You flea-bitten, flop-eared, sack of bones!" he shouted at his startled horse, giving it a cuff with his foot. Off and on in his miserable journey he had been taking his anger out on the only thing that could hear him—his horse. Just how the horse could be blamed might be a mystery, but the Jester blamed him anyway.

So, when the Jester slid off the horse's back to get a drink, the horse ambled away.

"Wait, stop! Come back!"

The Jester was after him in a minute, but the old horse had some spark left, and it ran down the trail, its dragging reins just a few feet out of reach. Having been used on inspection tours, it knew that it was closer to a barracks in the south than the one it had started from in the north. At last it outdistanced the Jester and left him panting on the trail, too winded to rant and rage.

A while later it came galloping easily past the woman and the Princess. It might have come if called to gently, for it was familiar with obedience to good masters, but even though Rosalynn wanted to pet it, the woman would not call to it.

"No, no, Princess, let it fly," she said. "It has somehow lost its rider and wants a safe stable for the night. We must not keep it out. It might meet wolves here at night and be pulled down by them."

"Wolves!" Rosalynn exclaimed, slipping her hand into the woman's. "Are there wolves here?"

"Oh, aye," she replied, looking down. Rosalynn sensed her gentle smile, though in the dusky woods the woman's hood shadowed most of her face. "Don't be afraid, Rosalynn. Wolves don't relish the taste of princess. They won't hurt you or me. They live mostly on jackrabbits and are content with those—though in a wilder country they could pull down a bull or moose, I'm sure."

"But how do you know?" Rosalynn asked.

"I've studied and learned. They may pause to watch us, but they'll avoid us. Only a very hungry wolf would attack a person." And she stroked Rosalynn's cheek. "We have nothing to fear—not from wolves, anyway." She led the Princess on, and soon the sounds of the horse's hooves died away on the path, and they were alone again.

At last, when absolutely no light penetrated through the trees, and the path became too difficult to be traveled at night, the woman groped along to a thicket, cleared it out, and led Rosalynn inside. She came in after her and closed it up.

Far away, a wolf howled. Another wolf, much closer, answered.

Rosalynn shivered and sat huddled against the woman. One wolf howl alone sounds sad and desolate, but when wolves howl in a group, they change their tones to howls and snarls, bellowings and sobbings that seem to curdle the blood. Now, as four or five voices joined in, Rosalynn couldn't resist whimpering and being afraid at the gibbering and shrieking. Many a full-grown warrior would have slept uneasily, with his hand on his sword.

But the woman said, "They are either forming a pack or arguing over a hunting ground. Don't be afraid— if they meant to hunt us they would be silent." And she wrapped her cloak around Rosalynn and sat for a while, rocking her in the darkness while Rosalynn strained her ears for the dreaded footfalls of approaching wolves and hid her face in the woman's gown.

But the woman was so relaxed and calm, and Rosalynn so tired from the hike, and the wolf howls growing so much more distant, that at last the Princess dozed and then slept. The woman laid her down, made sure she was well wrapped in the cloak, then watched awhile before falling asleep herself.

It was some hours later, after moonset and before sunrise, that Rosalynn heard something and opened her eyes. It was a man's voice.

"Oh me, oh me, oh me," it whimpered. "And to Rigel's own fool, too. Oh me, oh me, and wolves and no horse, no food—oh me—"

Rosalynn was about to wake the woman when the woman's warm and steady hand reached out and restrained her from sitting up. "I hear him, Rosalynn. Stay down," she whispered.

Rosalynn obeyed.

"He's alone," the woman whispered. "He doesn't sound like a soldier. In the morning we will meet him if he's still here."

Rosalynn woke again to a flaming pink and orange streak in the eastern sky. Dew hung on the leaves of the thicket. She lifted her head, but all was quiet.

The woman slowly sat up, watching through the leaves.

"He's asleep by the path," she murmured, slipping into her cloak. "Stay here."

"Nay!" Rosalynn seized her by the arm.

The eyes that had been unbearable for their kindness became terrible with sternness and shock at her words. "Do not disobey me," she said with a terrible voice that matched her eyes. Rosalynn winced and looked down.

"I mean to keep my promise. He may do you harm, and I mean to stay by you."

The terrible voice softened, though Rosalynn couldn't bear to meet those stern eyes again. "If I could not protect myself, Rosalynn, you could not protect me. Stay here, and I will have the power to protect both of us."

But Rosalynn hesitated. "I made a promise—"

"It is not the words themselves, but the spirit of love and honor that was promised," the woman said. "Obey me. Obey me," she repeated even more emphatically.

Her voice drew Rosalynn's eyes up, and Rosalynn bowed her head again under that powerful gaze, which was not stern anymore, but compelling and masterful.

"I will obey you."

"The most faithful of friends is the one who gives obedience. Don't cry." She kissed Rosalynn and went out into the forest.

Wiping away tears, Rosalynn peered through the leaves. She felt wretched.

In his sleep, the Fool sensed footsteps on the path. He jerked awake.

"Get back!" he cried at the hooded figure emerging from the shadows. "Mercy! Mercy!"

"You shall have mercy from me," she said, stepping into the sunny rays that penetrated through the trees. "I have never in my life denied mercy from any who has asked me for it."

When he saw she was only a woman, he straightened up.

"Who are you?" Then he leaped to his feet, as though threatening her, but he was shorter than she, for the woman was tall.

"Who are you?" he demanded.

"A traveler. A scholar. One who keeps a certain knowledge of medicine."

"I mean, what's your name?"

But she shook her head. "To those who know me I have names, but I don't give them out easily, not even one."

"Oh, you don't, eh? You high and gawking scarecrow!" He put his fists on his hips. "Now see here, you, no nonsense. I'm a rough man, and—"

She fixed him with one stare and walked away at a steady and measured pace down the path.

"Here now! Stop, I say! Stop, you!" and he chased her. "I said, Stop!" he screamed in a rage and threw a clawlike hand out to seize and hurt her. But she sidestepped, grabbed the wrist, and somehow the Jester found himself on his back once more, with the blue sky and green leaves above him.

He lifted his head and found her looking down at him from several paces away.

"That was quite foolish," she said. "As a physician I know the joints very well. It is a small thing to turn them into levers against each other."

"See here, I lost my temper." With a groan he sat up. "I didn't mean anything. I'm just hungry and footsore and lost. You took me by surprise, that's all."

"Then you should have asked me for food and directions," she replied.

He stood up, rubbing his lean and grizzled chin.

Her small pack of food was in her cloak. She took it out and threw it to him. "Take this," she said. "Follow this path along the river. With steady walking you should be in the village of Herrington late this afternoon—no!" She stretched out her hand to stop him from sitting down. "Go! Eat as you walk. That is the extent of my mercy. You may not stay here."

He had half a mind to argue, but when he considered how handily she had thrown him upside down, he decided to leave—for the present, at least. Grumbling, he walked away, cramming bread into his mouth.

She stayed on the path, watching him until at last he was a small figure through the trees, and then he was gone.

She hurried back to the thicket where Rosalynn sat waiting.

"It's safe," she said, "Come out."

A much quieter Rosalynn came out and went down to wash her face. After a moment, the woman followed her.

"I gave him our food to be rid of him," she said gently as Rosalynn splashed water onto her face.

"I am not afraid of starving, not with your knowledge of the forest," the Princess said without meeting the woman's eyes. Her face came up from the cold water, rosy and glowing, and she tried to seem cheerful.

"Come here, Rosalynn." The woman slipped her arms around Rosalynn. "I didn't mean to make you break your word," she said. "Nor do I reckon that your word has been broken, for when you gave me your promise you never intended that it should cause you to disobey me. Isn't that right?"

Rosalynn nodded.

"That man was a jester from Rigel's court. He may have taken you away or brought soldiers back. It was better for me to meet him alone."

"Are you angry with me?" Rosalynn asked.

"No. For this moment, obedience was required most of you, but the time will come, I'm sure, when you will prove the courage that you promised me."

Then she smiled at Rosalynn, and suddenly Rosalynn loved her even more and was glad she had obeyed.

Now the sky began to look sullen; the low gray bellies of swollen clouds crawled across the sky and met. Lower and lower they sank, while in the forest, mosquitoes came out. The flies drifted along more thickly, and the bees grew grumpy and fretful.

More and more often, the woman stopped at every clearing to watch the clouds.

"Will it be a bad storm?" Rosalynn asked at last.

"It looks bad. As you learned for yourself, the river is dangerous in a bad storm. And the land around Herrington is especially dangerous. It floods easily because it traps water. But we cannot go back. That Jester came from somewhere. It was not by chance that he was in these woods. Rigel has all his spare men searching for you. We must hurry to Herrington and row for the other shore where it will be safer."

So they hurried on, but not long after their conversation the clouds shed their rain and hurled lightning bolts across the sky. The river looked greenish and gray and sickly, ready to swell up in the downpour.

Rain poured down with a muffled roaring, and the leaves quickly gave up their fight to shed the water. They sagged down, pelted and torn by the sheets of water assaulting them. The path became slippery and difficult.

"The Herrington gully and stream bed will be flooded," the woman called over the waves of rain. "It will be hard to cross, but we'll have to do it."

Rosalynn could only give a short nod. She was weary, and struggling over the slick path made her even more weary.

They toiled on for several hours, until Rosalynn was too numb and tired to even sense much of where they were going or of how often the woman's arm had held her up by the hand when she would have slipped.

And then the ground sloped down to form a steep hill. The woman called to her.

"Are you all right?"

Rosalynn nodded and managed to look up. The woman smiled and said, "Almost there. Can you go on?"

Rosalynn rallied her strength and called back, "Aye. I can manage."

The trees cleared, and she saw a foaming and roaring flood in a gully below. The woman let out a sigh of chagrin. Jagged boulders, the remains of old landslides, lay half hidden in the foamy swirl, plentiful and dangerous.

"The footbridge must have been washed away," the woman said. "Or perhaps it is only submerged."

6
In Enemy Hands

They picked their way down closer to the foaming and churning flood. The woman scouted the lip of the gully, searching. At last she found what she wanted.

"See," she said to Rosalynn, whose hand she had not let go all this time. She pointed to several firmly staked pegs embedded in the rocks and all but covered in the flood. "This is the footbridge—submerged. But the people here are used to floods. The men have devised a way to cross even in flood, though it isn't pleasant."

She led Rosalynn up a little way to the trees and found a big oak with an opening in its trunk.

"This looks likely. It's not been dead long," she said. "And it's been hollowed out. These are hatchet marks along the natural opening." She reached inside and drew out two coils of line. One line she wrapped twice around the base of the tree and secured it.

"Come," she said, and they went back to the footbridge with the woman unwinding the coil of rope as she went.

It was a light rope, yards and yards long, made with a craft and cunning not equaled on the Bracken side of the river.

"Study it well," the woman said, and Rosalynn felt the gravity in her voice. "It stores easily, is light, and could hold back the power of an ox. We can trust our lives to it, and we must. All of Folger could trust itself to this rope, and to the craftsmanship of its people, whom hardship has taught good craft. Yet for want of land they ever fight their neighbors."

Rosalynn looked up at her. But the woman was busy knotting one of the ropes.

"Now for our crossing," she said. "I will go first, holding the rope and finding the footbridge with my feet. Do you see those twin rocks?"

She pointed ahead at two jutting peaks thrust up through the flooded gully. "The footbridge cuts between them, and the floor of the gully quickly rises beyond them so that the waters soon become shallow. Then there will be land and trees again. I will go ahead with this guide rope, through the boulders and up the other side and fasten the line. Then we can cross together, using our hands on the guide rope and our feet on the footbridge. Wait for me."

Rosalynn nodded. The woman removed cloak and shoes, hitched up the light traveling garment to her knees, and—with the spare coil over her left shoulder—entered the roaring torrent with her hands paying out the guide rope.

Her feet were on the footbridge, but as soon as she was out to her chin a strong current swept into her. Her head disappeared a moment, then came up, and Rosalynn knew from the position of the woman's head that she was swimming, with her right hand holding the guide rope, and her left hand down beneath, holding some part of the footbridge, probably a handrail made of rope.

She submerged again and reappeared farther away. Rosalynn decided that she was using her feet, too, to help her shinny along the handrail of the footbridge while she paid out the guide rope.

Then at last she was at the twin peaks, two collapsed sentinels made of fallen rock from previous floods and landslides. She stopped there, steadying herself against one pillar of rock while she spliced her second coil of rope to the first. Then at last she went on, disappearing beyond the narrow opening between the boulders.

Rosalynn, bent on watching the woman's progress, didn't hear the footsteps behind her. Suddenly she was pulled off her feet and held pinned against somebody's chest with one wiry arm.

"Let me go!" she cried. "Let go!"

It was the Jester, his wizened and grizzled face slicked down in the pouring rain. His free arm gripped a savage soldier's knife. Up it flashed and then came down as it slashed through the guide rope that was the woman's life line.

"No!" Rosalynn screamed. "She'll drown! Don't do it!"

It flashed again, and the guide rope snapped.

Rosalynn struggled furiously and suddenly was flung down against the rocks. Breathless and stunned, she lay for several minutes without seeing anything. When her senses returned, she saw him emerge, dripping, from the stakes. He had cut the ropes on the footbridge, too.

He pinned her to the rocks with his knee and hesitated. She knew he was making up his mind, weighing the advantages of bringing her dead or alive back to his master. At last he yanked her to her feet and pulled her up the hill through the pouring rain.

It was quieter in the trees, where the downpour was muffled.

"Now quit yer blubbin'," he said. He yanked down a piece of wet vine. "Or you'll get a taste of this on your back. C'mere anyway!" And he used the tough and fibrous vine as a rope to tie her hands behind her back. "Now yer precious majesty," he said, "there's outposts along this way, and we'll find one soon enough. Then it's high times for you, all right. Kill her quick—don't torture her, Varger says. Only I'm the one that's bringing you in. Now move along! Say—"And his words stopped her. He squinted at the silence which she had fallen into so readily. "You seem awful agreeable. If yer planning anything, give it up. D'you hear?"

"I have no plans," she said. Her voice was high, but clear. "Only I know that you have struck down and killed a noble woman. As surely as we stand here you will pay for having slain her. Your life is worthless." And despite herself, the Princess trembled with rage and grief.

For a moment he stared at her, astonished, then he held his lean belly and laughed. "And who might make me pay?" he asked. "You? Oh, you're a good one—still a child! No, Princess, there's nothing *I* fear that's going to—"

A stout club tapped the back of his head. With a sigh he slipped to the forest floor.

Instantly the wet forest was filled with howls of glee. Ragged men and women darted from behind trees and descended on the Fool. Some dug their hands into his pockets. A man and woman wrestled to get his boots off. Others yanked his cape free. Someone snatched up his knife and groped along his belt for the sheath.

In the next instant, several more descended on Rosalynn. They pulled her this way and that, tore out her pockets in search of money, pulled on her hair, poked, pinched, and squeezed her.

She couldn't struggle with her hands tied behind her back, and every time she kicked at them, they howled with glee at her, as young vagabonds might laugh when tormenting a puppy. They twitched at her hair and clothes to make her turn this way and that.

Then suddenly one rugged man in better clothes than the others snatched her up under one brawny arm and began clouting heads this way and that with his free hand as though he were swatting flies.

"Enough! Enough!" he bellowed as though they were unruly children. He held Rosalynn pinned at such an angle that she could see that his whole face was wrapped in a crude bandage, except for one brown eye that glared both valiantly and carelessly down at his cronies.

One of the men drew a knife, but her captor was quicker. Like a cat, he leaped back, his own knife drawn, his strong legs tensed to dash in and out and fight. He shifted Rosalynn so that his arm pinned her closer to his back, out of the way of his fight. But his attacker turned coward and put the knife away.

"Let our King choose her fate!" the bandaged man said. "To the council hall!" They paused, but the anger passed from their faces, and they agreed with a shout. And they trooped off just as readily as they had attacked, leaving the Fool behind like a picked-over chicken in the dimpling puddles of water and mud—bootless, penniless, weaponless, and capeless.

Once on the move in the driving rain, the bandits paid little heed to Rosalynn. But now that they ignored her, her captor gently cradled her in his arms instead of keeping her so roughly pinned. He drew his cloak around her—whether to hide her from prying eyes or to protect her from the rain, she didn't know.

The vines still burned her arms, and she couldn't help crying a little from the pain and from her shock. But he let her shift her weight to ease her burning wrists. At first, he watched straight ahead with his uncovered eye and scanned on either side, furtively watching the others while water soaked into the already sodden bandage or streamed down the few bare patches of his face. But as a rainy darkness fell, Rosalynn began to doze despite her fear, and when she woke up with a start at having been asleep, she saw that his one eye was looking down at her. His good eye seemed sorrowful, she thought, and she dared to speak.

"What will you do with me?" she asked him.

"Don't fear me, P—" he began, then cut his sentence off.

He had almost called her *Princess*. "But how does he know?" she asked herself.

"Don't fear me," he said again. "I would die before harming one hair of your golden head. But my strength cannot save you from the Robber Band. I must devise your rescue with cunning. Pardon me for what I do, but any jewel that you wear may cost you your life." And he took the royal jewel from her with a single, deft snap of its chain. She gasped, but he whispered. "I shall deliver it back to your hands, O lady." Then he said no more, but she began to hope again.

At last the band came to a grove, and inside there was a clearing, sheltered by trees.

The rain had slowed to a drizzle, and the grove was sheltered as well as if it had been roofed. Rain could not pierce the thick canopy of trees.

Slatternly robber wives scurried here and there with dry wood that had been stored under thatch. After a few moments a roaring fire blazed up in the center of the clearing. Skinned rabbits were put upright on skewers to roast, and potatoes pilfered from farms and gardens were thrust into the hot ashes.

The one-eyed man had held her close through all this, but she felt the robbers eyeing her. Then at last somebody must have signaled him, for he gingerly set her down and cut the vines binding her numb hands.

"Bring the wench! Bring the wench!" several cried, and she was snatched from him, pushed forward to the fire, then up along the side of it, until she stood before the Robber King, who sat on a throne made of logs. He was fat and sloppy, but not without signs of intelligence.

He eyed her in a long moment of silence, and during that time the one-eyed man slunk around the outside of the grove and came out by the throne where he would be near her. He stood with one hand on the knife at his belt, and his single eye gazed from Robber King to Princess and back again. She had the idea that if things went against her, he would fight for her, regardless of how hopeless it would be. Despite the one-eyed man's courage, Rosalynn trembled before the Robber King. Her fear seemed to please him.

"What be you doing tra'passing our woods?" the Robber King asked.

"I was trying to go to Herrington," Rosalynn said.

"Why so?"

"My guardian was taking me there. That man whom your people overwhelmed slew her in the flood and snatched me up to kidnap me." Despite herself, her voice shook again in her account of the wise woman's death.

"Ah! A villain *he* was!" the Robber King roared, laughing. "Good thing we saved you, eh?" Then he eyed her again. "Ah, you ain't dressed for Folger. Be you one of them knowledgeable folk from upriver?"

"My guardian was such," she replied. "I am no scholar such as she was."

"But you are booklearned?"

"Yes." And she explained no more.

"Well, then. Somebody wants you back, then, some rich kin of yours. If you can be ransomed, you have naught to fear from us."

She hesitated, but she knew that if she gave herself away, they would sell her to Rigel. And there were a hundred bits of vital information that Rigel could glean from her before he executed her. So she was silent.

"*No* one?" he asked, eyes wide.

"My father is far away in Bracken," she said. "You could never reach him."

"You bear yourself uncommon brave," he said at last. Then he called to the others. "We must do something with her then."

The whole crowd of them started up with a shout, like dogs after a rabbit. But he silenced them with a wave of his dagger and a roar.

"None o' that just yet!" he bellowed. "We takes suggestions one at a time! One at a time!"

They quieted down but stood around the fire watching her hungrily. Rosalynn's knees trembled under her wet dress and torn cloak, but she kept her head up.

"Couples first," the Robber King said. "Now here's a young'n what's booklearned and pretty fair. What man and wife will adopt her, eh? Come, speak up! Look at her, at least!"

Nobody said anything. After a moment a dirty man and his ragged wife pushed forward to look at her, then moved away. Another couple came, and another. But they all moved away, and Rosalynn was glad. They looked either savage or shrewd or both, and she knew that being "adopted" would mean living as a slave, suffering starvation and whippings, and being taught to steal, which she promised herself she would never do, whatever the consequence.

"What's wrong with you?" the King bellowed when the eight robber-husbands and robber-wives had looked her over and patted her ripped garments for anything left to steal.

"Too genteel," one man said gruffly. "It's stamped on her face. She'd kick too much and die in the traces, like as not."

"Well, keep her and sell her as a wife later on!" the King roared. "Some ugly noble would pay dear for her in five years or so! Man, he would pay enough to buy a cottage in Bracken and live at ease."

"Deals like that takes brains," another man said. "Which ain't plentiful around here. Stealing's easier."

And the others nodded. One of the wives fingered her knife. "Of course, the little morsel *is* tender yet, and passable plump," she began, but the one-eyed robber interrupted.

"Ho! I'll take her," he said quickly.

The King frowned at him. "What for?"

"To take her to Bracken and get a ransom for her," he said.

"Are you mad? You'll never come back!"

"Well, it's my choice, and it beats killing a child that's been booklearned!"

Some of the robbers nodded. They weren't soft-hearted, but they feared meddling with high-class people. Getting rid of her safely and at another person's expense suited them exactly. But others resisted. They were bored and restless. Tormenting the helpless was their pleasure, and they didn't want to give up a game so quickly. They argued.

"I defend my claim with my life," the one-eyed man said. "Whoever wishes to claim her, let him come and fight me." And he threw his cape off and drew his dagger.

The robbers greeted this with a shout of glee and would have rushed him, but the King's bellow halted them.

"One at a time," he ordered.

"But he's too young and strong!" one of them protested.

"Well said! Two at a time," the King agreed.

The one-eyed man picked up his cape in his left hand and twirled it around his left arm to ward off knife blows. Two thinner, ragged men rushed forward to meet him, when the intense silence of the crowd was broken by a shout.

"Stop!"

All but the three fighters looked up. They continued to eye each other. But in a moment even they looked at the gray figure approaching.

Rosalynn started, almost fearfully. "Oh, my mistress!" she cried.

The robbers abruptly drew back from the figure, and the Robber King looked uneasy, for they were one and all superstitious and fearful, and they had heard Rosalynn testify that the woman had drowned.

Now she stood before the Robber King, her face lost in the cowl, her cloak streaming water from the rain.

"Why have you stolen my ward?" she asked.

"Well, uh, be you so good to explain where you've come from, madam," the King said.

"From the flooded gully. Why have you stolen my ward?"

He hesitated, looking more and more uneasy. "W-well—w-we—"

"Answer me."

His voice sank to a whisper. "We thought—be you drowned?"

"Foolish and dark of heart!" she exclaimed. "All your life you look over your shoulder for those you have killed, because you know your own wickedness. How well you know what punishments await you—" Here the Robber King turned miserably pale, as though every word she spoke pierced him. "I have not drowned. I overcame the waters. I will overcome you, if I must. Give me the girl!"

"W-well, if water don't withstand you, I w-won't. You upriver folks know your own ways. Y-you just take her. J-just take her. W-we ain't done her no harm. W-we almost adopted her. This gentleman here—"

"Silence!' she commanded, and he stopped. "Hear me," she said. "You robbers subject yourselves to dark fancies and burn your fires high at night because of your fears. But if you continue so, no fire shall drive away your superstitious fears, though that fire burn forever! Come, Rosalynn."

Rosalynn took the offered hand in both of hers, and they left the grove.

"Quick! In the darkness they may avenge themselves!" the woman whispered. "This way!" And they scurried down a maze of paths, their gray cloaks hiding them in the dark woods.

7
Herrington

The two marched half the night and crossed the dangerous gully in a skiff. Then the woman must have carried her into Herrington, for the Princess had no memory after crossing the flood.

She woke up to find herself rolled snugly in a warm blanket. Her clothes were hung on a rack by the fireplace across the room. And the woman—dressed in her own newly dried clothes—was tending the fire. She saw that Rosalynn was awake and came to her.

First there was a welcome hug, and for a moment Rosalynn forgot everything else but being safe with the wise woman. She didn't even care about the journey ahead, just the happiness of being together. Then the Princess asked, "How did you get away from the gully? I thought you were drowned."

"I almost was," the woman said. "When my guide rope snapped, I was just coming up for air and couldn't get a hold on anything. Then the bridge was cut loose, so I had to strike out for the shore on my side of the rocks. But it was close, and the rocks broke up the swiftness of the current, once I got away from them.

By and by I made it, and I found some skiffs put out for people to cross with. I crossed again and found the Fool and the trail of the bandits. So I followed it. Now tell me what happened to *you.*"

Then while the woman petted her and smoothed her hair, Rosalynn told her side of the story.

"Well, it was horrible," the woman said at the end. "But we are both of us alive and well at the end of it. Such savage folk! They will hinder Rigel's men also, I hope."

"The one-eyed man wasn't savage," Rosalynn said. "He was gallant."

"To you, anyway," the woman agreed. "If you feel ready, you may dress. Your clothes are dry and mended. Our supper will be here soon."

Rosalynn obeyed. No sooner was she finished dressing in her mended clothes than someone knocked. "Supper!" a man's voice called. The woman let in a steward so laden with dishes that they came higher than his face.

"Supper!" the woman exclaimed as he staggered in with it, his face still hidden. "It's a feast!"

"That's because you have a guest," the steward said, and lowered the tray to the trestle table by the fire.

Rosalynn gasped. "The robber!"

The one-eyed man bowed to her and then knelt on one knee. "My Princess," he said gravely. "Forgive my frivolity. Allow me to pledge to you my loyalty now and forever! Long live your house! Long reign your father, my King!" And from his ragged tunic he brought out the royal jewel and gave it back to her.

Rosalynn stepped forward, and the woman closed the door.

"Who are you?" the Princess asked.

"Know you not your own true servant?" he asked tenderly. "I am Herron, your rider."

"Herron!" and she flung herself into his arms as he knelt there on one knee. Now she recognized his manner, gestures, even the one eye that showed through the bandage.

"Herron!" she sobbed. "Forgive me! Forgive me! For every foolish word I said in the saddle that day, forgive me, Herron!" And she cried bitterly on his shoulder.

"Dear Princess, I forgive you," he said. "And sooth, last night when I saw your queenly courage and modesty before that rabble, my heart thrilled. You've grown to be a true princess, my dear, and right gladly would I have fought for you last night. Nay, so long ago when I rebuked you, my heart still yearned over you, for I loved my Princess then as now."

Then he shifted her to his other shoulder where she cried again and hugged his neck. "Many days did I search for you, my Princess, once I recovered from the wounds that Rigel's darts dealt me. His men left me for dead, but a poor farmer riding homeward found me and took me home. He and his wife bound me up and cared for me. My only grief is my left eye, which is infected from a gash it received of some twigs when I fell," he said. "It was my least wound at first, and now the worst. I bandaged my face up along with the eye to hide my identity from Rigel's men, should they have seen me. Then I joined myself to bandits in his country to wreak havoc here and scout for you. I heard you had been seen on this side of the Bridge."

She straightened up. "Did you rob people?" she asked.

"No, not one," he said. "I mostly spied on the soldiers and set a few outposts by the river on fire. I robbed *their* larders, because that's spoils of war." Then he kissed her cheek and stood up.

"I will look at your eye," the woman said. She moved a chair by the fire. "Sit here."

While Rosalynn set the table, the woman unwrapped Herron's clumsy bandage, revealing two scars on his handsome face and an eye badly swollen from infection.

It was almost funny to see Herron, the big rider and gallant robber, sit meekly on a stool while the woman washed his face and bathed his eye and reproached him for using dirty bandages.

She set a poultice on it and wrapped the poultice into place. Then they all sat down to eat.

All three were hungry and ate in silence. But Herron ate longest, falling to on roast chicken, mashed potatoes, stewed carrots, and baked apples with a zest that betrayed long, hungry days in the forest.

"When I am queen, he shall not want for anything," Rosalynn promised herself. "For he has endured every hardship in the faint hope of finding me here."

"Now we must plan," the woman said when at last he had pushed back his plate and taken up his mug of steaming tea.

"Well, if you please, Mother," he asked the woman, "I should like to know who you are—a friend of the Princess here in Folger. It's unusual."

So the woman explained their story.

"All the realm of Bracken is in your debt," he said when she'd finished. "I put myself at your service—what do you wish? Bodyguard? Oarsman? Spy? I shall stay with you or do your bidding. Only ask me."

The wise woman smiled, and for the first time Rosalynn truly saw her age. Keen of eye she might be, strong of hand and great of heart she had proved, but next to her, the rugged Herron was a boy. No wonder he had given her the respectful title of Mother. He felt the difference in age between himself and the woman as clearly as Rosalynn did.

"I have a plan," she said. "It will delay my journey with the Princess, but it may save Bracken. Do you know the song that the castle guard sing?"

He nodded. "I've heard it, but it was never my place to learn it all."

"Then I will sing it for you," she said. "And I want you to listen and tell me what it says:

Come war, the soldier earns his trade
Beat the drums; my heart inspire.
Bring me my iron blade,
My helmet rivet on.
Bring me the prancing horse.
Gird on my sword of fire.

Nay, come there many boots
On cobblestones that ring?
Disarm me where the waters course.
My iron helm unhinge.
A riverboat shall be my horse.
One axe shall overthrow a king.

In the night the soldier creeps
Midway from shore to shore
High above the murky deep
On the slender wooden floor.
'Twill one man safely keep,
Whose axe shall end a war."

He inclined his head as she finished. "Well sung, but what purpose does it serve?"

"Do you know anything of its meaning?" the woman asked.

"I had always heard it was a song of a warrior's urge to save Bracken by land or sea," Herron told her. "Yet it sounds like the soldier in the song first desires to go to war, and then when he hears that there are many boots marching toward him, he throws off all his armor and rows away on the river."

"And the last verse?" the woman asked.

Herron frowned. "The last verse—I would say—is describing some kind of outpost. An outpost on a tower above the river. For what else could 'a slender wooden floor' placed 'high above the murky deep' serve for?" He shook his head.

"Do you think that makes sense?" the woman asked him.

"Folk songs often fail to make sense, and this one seems to be out of order. First the soldier wants to fight; then he wants to leave; then he finds himself doing sentry duty on a tower that does not exist." Herron shrugged. "I give up."

"In the middle verse, I don't think he is abandoning his army," the woman told him. "I think he is choosing to trade all his armor for a riverboat and axe. For throughout the song he never loses his belief that one axe will overthrow a king. He maintains it to the very end."

"Perhaps he means to chop down the Bridge." And Herron couldn't hide a smile on that, but when the woman didn't acknowledge the joke, he became alarmed. "Come now, nobody could do that! It would take an army, and even then they would be hailed with arrows and boiling tar while they tried to work!"

"I did not say an army could do it. An army could not do it. The song says that one axe shall end the war."

"But it's just a song!"

"No, it isn't. It was given to the castle guard generations ago, preparing it for such a time when one great warlord would seek to overrun Bracken. Don't you see that the soldier in the song is ready to fight until he learns that the army he must fight is big? Then he turns to the river, and he throws away his sword. There's strategy in that. He's singing of his plan."

Herron nodded. "Well, there's only one wooden place on the whole river, and that's the Bridge. But I've never been under it. I don't know what it looks like except from a distance. Yet even so, I would say that no single man could chop it down."

"It has pillars," Rosalynn put in. "Huge pillars set in sockets of stone. And the pillars are coated with tar."

"I wonder," the woman said. "Could a person climb one of those pillars:

Midway from shore to shore
High above the murky deep
On the slender wooden floor
'Twill one man safely keep,"

she repeated softly to herself. "Is there a pillar midway from shore to shore? And is there a platform where a man might stand?"

"There may be a trick floor that can be swung down from a hiding place," Herron admitted. "There were secret platforms like that in the castle where hidden archers were to be posted. I suppose the same could have been done on the Bridge."

"And there is also a key crossbeam," the woman told him.

Herron shrugged. "A support beam geared to hold up one solid piece of the Bridge? Aye, such there might be—and it's clear to me that you think there is. If that support were weakened or cut through, part of the Bridge would fall. But it would take more than one man just the same. Even a single crossbeam on the Bridge would be huge."

"Most of them, yes," she said. "But the Bridge is a suspension bridge. It hangs from the high pillars by cables, does it not? Every time a big army marches across it, the army would cause even that big bridge to sway. The repetition of feet causes a buildup of force that the Bridge was designed to withstand. If only one section were weakened—one small section—that one weak area that failed to do its part would put stress on the rest of the Bridge—"

"How do you know these things?" he asked her.

"Because I am learned in my country's history. It was my countrymen—centuries ago—that built the Bridge. Parts of the song of the castle guard have been lost; yet I feel sure of my interpretation if you are willing to trust me. I believe that somewhere on that Bridge there is a smaller supporting beam, or perhaps a mere pin giving support to a larger beam—something small enough for one man to chop through."

"You have not really been asking me these things, then," Herron said. "Only trying to convince me."

"Aye. I must know that you believe in me before I ask you to go with me. Are you willing to think I am right in this?"

"I am. You make me believe it must be so. We must try it!" Herron exclaimed.

"Is Rigel's main invasion force amassed yet?" the woman asked.

"No. He and the King of Bracken are playing a spying game right now. Half of Rigel's forces are stationed here in Folger for attack or defense. Once his spies confirm the King's plans, Rigel will send his forces over the Bridge. They will go out to meet the King's resistance and crush him." Herron shook his head. "Alas, when we did not defend the Bridge in the first evening, we lost all Bracken to Rigel. The Bridge has ever been the key to our weakness."

"We may yet dismay Rigel," the woman said. "If we're right about the clues in the song. I must visit the ironmonger directly."

"Very well, Mother. And me?"

"It is the time of the spring rains," she said. "Ideal for us to move. Can you ready a skiff for us?"

"Aye."

"We have walked barely thirty miles since leaving my cottage. Tonight we may row upriver as far as we dare, and tomorrow night, attack the Bridge. Come back here in two hours, and we shall leave in secret."

Herron bowed and left.

The evening passed slowly. Together the Princess and the woman went out into the wet streets to make their purchases—two axes and several burlap sacks.

Then the woman put Rosalynn back to bed. Rosalynn was sure she wasn't tired, and she lay with her eyes wide open and alert. Only the river lay between her and home; yet now they would be pushing north again, recovering their long journey.

Meanwhile, the woman gathered their things. She packed the leftovers of their fine supper into several small parcels and left the money for their bed and board on the table.

She lighted a lamp and banked the fire, packed their things into a bundle, stood the axes against the table, and sat down to wait. Rosalynn tried to keep her eyes open, to focus them on the gray figure outlined in the glow of the lamp, but the room wavered, and the figure went out of focus. The light dimmed and came back again as she struggled to stay awake.

Then suddenly there were bandits all along the walls, shouting with glee at her, and the woman was gone.

"One at a time! One at a time!" A voice cried, but they were surging toward her.

All of a sudden there was the woman bending over her, saying, "It's all right. You've been dreaming, that's all. You'll rest better with me."

And she let Rosalynn sit up with her, leaning against her and wrapped up in the blankets and her arms. Rosalynn wondered what would happen after it was all over—after they arrived at the Duke's castle. Would the woman stay? Or would she return to the little cottage? Rosalynn would never be able to return there, not safely, anyway. She wondered if they would ever see each other again. And in thinking those thoughts she put her arms around the woman and hugged her. But she didn't ask her to stay in Bracken. It didn't seem fair to whoever else would stumble to the cottage door. And besides, the woman, Rosalynn decided, would love her equally from far away or nearby.

At last Herron came with news that he had a skiff. They gathered up their belongings, and the woman blew out the lamp.

The rain had stopped for a while. Heavy, dismal fog hung over everything, and even though it was spring, Rosalynn could see her breath in the air. The streets were still except for the sound of water dripping in drainpipes. Moisture clung to the damp wooden sides of the squarely built houses. Here and there cheerful lights glowed in the windows, or lanterns bobbed past on the main streets.

It was a fishing village, and so the people were more prosperous than in the other parts of Folger farther from the river. But at the same time a kind of gloom hung on everything, for most of the men were away at the war. The streets were quiet.

There were watchmen along the harbor, looking out for refugees or enemy troops from across the river. Herron, with a green cape thrown over his tattered green leggings and tunic, guided them to a pile of lumber near the pier, and they waited behind it until the watchman went by on his rounds.

They scuttled to the pier and went down a ladder: the woman first, to help the Princess, then Rosalynn, then Herron last of all. Then they sat very quietly in the damp stillness. They heard the watchman go by again, his eyes looking out over the river. After he was gone, the woman and Herron quickly wrapped the oars in the burlap sacks. Then again they were silent. They heard the boards of the pier creak as the watchman went by.

At last, with silent, strong pulls, Herron rowed them out. The woman and the Princess stayed low, their hoods pulled over their faces. Herron's hood was down, too. They were quickly skimming out of the circle of light from the town and the fishing harbor. In a moment they were out of the range of eyesight in the dark and foggy night.

But Herron continued to pull silently, and Rosalynn didn't make a noise, knowing full well that sound would travel far over the quiet waters. Then at last there were only trees and brush on every side. The fog lifted after a while, but the night sky was inky with swollen clouds. Not a gleam of starlight or moonlight shone through them.

Now the woman came alongside Herron, and they both pulled against the current, both silent, and keeping to the middle of the wide river. They rowed well together, the woman pacing herself and Herron keeping down to her pace. Rosalynn kept a watch on the bank and back toward Herrington, making sure that they hadn't been followed. It was a tedious night—of the splashing of the water against the wooden bow, and the creaking of the oarlocks as they strained against a contrary current; of the straining to see or hear an enemy; of straining to sit up on the hard bench because the dripping burlap sacks had been flung on the bottom of the boat now that absolute silence was unnecessary.

Finally Rosalynn fell into a kind of waking doze—listening and looking without really seeing or hearing anything. But anything out of the ordinary would have roused her at once.

At last Herron told the woman to rest a little, and she sat by Rosalynn and watched for her, rubbing the Princess's aching back and letting her rest a little. Then the woman spelled Herron, and he took Rosalynn's watch for her, drawing his cape over her in the chill night. She could feel how tense he was. Even while he rowed he listened and watched, and every now and then he directed that the boat should be moved farther out from the Folger shore.

Conquered or enemy territory was on either side right now, but since neither country had mastered sailing or the use of large ships, the only thing they had to fear was skiffs their own size, which they could outdistance if they only spotted pursuit quickly enough.

At long, long last, they rowed in to the Folger side under a clump of slender willows. After some silent struggle they got the skiff under the willows, and the woman made the willows into a sort of screen for the boat. Herron took some food from the parcels and went up onto the bank to roost in a tree and keep an eye out for patrols.

The woman and the Princess ate some of the cold food, but they were both too weary to eat much. They huddled together on the side of the boat opposite the wet sacks and sank into sleep.

A sullen dawn came. They drank and ate a little, but it wasn't safe to talk when they couldn't watch for enemies, so they soon fell asleep again.

Toward late afternoon they woke up again and waited for the darkness to fall and for Herron to come back down. They watched the twilight fall over the dusky river, and far away they could hear the pounding of the stonecutters ringing up and down on the waters, until at last it was too dark for the men, and all was still. The bullfrogs started, and whippoorwills were chanting their rhythmic calls. A strong breeze picked up over the river, signaling more rain. At long last, when the sky was too dark to separate from the riverbank on the other shore, Herron came.

He slid into the skiff, and Rosalynn surprised and pleased him with a kiss on his cheek.

"Sooth, I had half forgotten my sweet child Princess in the face of my queenly Princess," he said with a small chuckle. "You are still my little girl, Princess?"

She nodded. "Of course I am."

But then he shook his head. "Nay, you are growing up too much. You will see for yourself when we get home. And when you put away all your childish toys, Princess, don't forget the rider who served you of old and will gladly serve you all his days," he said seriously.

"I had already reminded myself of your hard labor, Herron," she said, with so much dignity and grace that he bowed his head. And suddenly she realized that she *had* changed a little inside herself since the day when he had scolded her on his saddle.

It had been more pleasant, she decided, when he'd simply played with her and spoiled her than when he bowed to her and vowed to serve her.

"Yet all along he has served me," she thought with a little shock. "Even when he played with me and then when he scolded me."

There was no time to think further, for they were silently pushing out, using one of the oars as a pole to get away from the bank.

Now Herron and the woman could change places less frequently because they were constantly passing outposts on one bank or the other, and the river was narrower here. Any motion, any sound, might alert a patrol.

About an hour after they started, a light rain began to fall. Soon it became heavier until it was a downpour. Both Herron and the woman strained against the choppy waves of the river. It was stirred up by the wind and resisted harder than ever.

They didn't have to be so quiet in the noise of the rain beating the river, and it was a good thing, because the tired old skiff groaned and creaked under the stress.

There was no thought of pacing now. Both Herron and the woman pulled each pull of the oars with all they were worth, trying to keep in time with each other and get to the next stroke. The skiff rode up a swell, and waves splashed over the prow.

"How far?" Rosalynn heard him gasp to her. "How far do you reckon it?"

But from the woman there was only a sharp sigh of breath and then a quick intake as she strained on the oar.

Herron let out an exclamation. "You're exhausted! Let me take it! Let me take it for you!"

"No. Pull! A league maybe from here—not far—"

And then the woman's voice was lost as she pulled on her oar.

The moments that followed were tense and silent as they struggled against the rebellious waters. Rosalynn was so worried for the woman that she lost track of the time, and it seemed like a sudden thing to see the Bridge looming above them up ahead in the dark and rainy night.

"There!" the Princess whispered.

At the same moment the wind slackened sharply, and the rain eased a little. With renewed strength the woman and Herron pulled for it.

Even in the rainy night, the pillars of the Bridge stood silhouetted against the sky behind them.

"Aim us for the middle pillar," the woman gasped. " 'Midway from shore to shore,' " she quoted.

8

The Bridge and What Followed

They anchored at a central pillar. The woman tried to rise to climb out onto the base of the stone socket, but she fell back. Herron caught her. "It only calls for one axe, Mother," he said to her. "I'll climb up and do it."

"Are there handholds?" she asked.

"I'll see." He eased her back onto the bottom of the skiff. Next he took off his warm cloak—still dry on the inside—and wrapped it around her. He could feel a stickiness on her hands where they had bled from the hard wooden oars, and for a moment he wondered how to make her comfortable.

"Herron," she asked. "Why are you waiting? Is something wrong?"

"I—no," he said. "Rosalynn, can you help me?"

"Yes."

They took an axe from the skiff and climbed onto the base of the huge stone socket. Herron managed to shinny up it, gripping it where he had to and finding handholds on some of the mortared rock. Rosalynn watched from below as he reached the pillar of wood. He stood on the stone ledge of the socket and inched his way around it. Over the noise of the waves pounding the forest of stone sockets under the Bridge, she thought she heard him gasp.

He came shinnying down. "There *are* handholds in there," he said. "Strips of tarred wood have been pegged into this pillar on the north side where nobody would see them from the shore or from above. I think they'll hold me."

Rosalynn helped him sling the axe through the back of his belt, and then he climbed up again. This time he went higher, climbing up the secret ladder.

Rosalynn dropped lightly into the skiff. "There *are* handholds, mistress," she said to the woman. "He's gone up."

They waited for what seemed like an hour while the rain beat down on the waters around the Bridge and the waves lapped against the boat and the stone sockets of the pillars. The woman, spent from struggling upriver in the storm, leaned against Rosalynn and waited with her.

At last Rosalynn could hear him coming down hand over hand. He shinnied down the socket, landed at the base, and leaped into the skiff.

"I climbed until the handholds ran out," he said, "and there was a false handhold of some sort. I could tell when I felt it that it wouldn't hold my weight. But when I pulled on it, a flet—a light platform—dropped down into place. I climbed onto it, and from there I could feel a single crossbeam—not very sturdy, either, and so I chopped it through with my axe—just like the song told us. At first I didn't hear or see anything, but then I heard a creaking—a creaking. That crossbeam was a pin fastening a beam that anchors a couple of the cables. When I cut through it, it loosened the beam, I think. It may work. It has to work!"

"Cut us loose," the woman said. "We can make twenty miles downriver in this gale."

He cut loose and stayed at the oars only to keep the boat in the middle of the river. The woman rested with the Princess.

Dawn found them on the Bracken side of the river, back in territory still patrolled by Bracken men from the castle of the Duke of Small. They landed at the first little fishing village they found, and Herron took them to an inn.

For an hour the innkeeper and his wife bustled about to take care of the wise woman, whom they took for a noble lady escaped from the battle in the north. They washed her hands of blood and cleaned out the splinters, then they laid her in their best bed and sent in soup and tea and other nourishing food.

"She needs only rest," Herron told Rosalynn as they stood at her bedside. "If you can spare me, Princess," and he knelt on one knee. "It is my duty to bring good news of your rescue to your father and to inform him of all that has passed. The Duke's castle is barely two miles off. Men shall be sent to escort you to it."

"As you please, Herron," she said to him. "You must go where your duty leads you. Only come back to me safe. That is my request. And tell my gracious father how earnestly I wish to see him."

He kissed her hand, bowed to her, and left quickly. Rosalynn turned back to the woman, who was sleeping. There was nothing to do but wait.

But suddenly the silence was interrupted by a hammering on the door. It burst open from the other side.

"What is the meaning of this?" Rosalynn asked as two of her uncle's soldiers marched in, followed by a captain.

"Did you and two companions land in this town from the river?" the captain asked her.

"We did."

"Then you must be detained as enemy aliens. Put the woman in chains, men, and keep a guard on the girl."

"Halt! I am the Princess Rosalynn, and whoso lays a violent hand on me shall answer with his life to the King!"

The soldiers drew back, and Rosalynn pulled out her proof of royalty, the jewel that hung around her neck. Instantly the two soldiers removed their helmets and knelt, and the captain, after a moment, uncovered his head and bowed. "I beg your majesty's pardon," he said. "It is as you say. Yet not a soul in the land knows of your whereabouts. Have you truly been hiding in Folger?"

"I was trying to escape from Folger, Captain, and this woman gave me my aid and—"

One of the soldiers looked up. "From Folger?" he roared, and drew his sword.

"Stop! She has saved my life!" Rosalynn exclaimed, and the soldier stopped, but his eyes stayed fixed on the woman's throat as though he would have liked to do away with her on the spot.

"She must be arrested at once," the captain said. "Pardon me, your majesty. It is your father's order."

"She's no enemy. She's not even of Folger. She only lived there—"

"Your majesty, his orders stand—sick or not, helpful or not. Do you not know how the armies of Rigel have slain every last person in your father's castle and burned out village after village? More horrors stalk day to day through our land than can be spoken of. And this woman comes from that accursed land," he said. "I vow to you, your highness, I would be hanged at once if I spared her from the prison."

For a moment the Princess was at a loss, but then she rallied herself. "You must do your duty, Captain, but I also have a duty. Rigel's men were on me, as close to me as you are yourself, and this woman saved my life and took me in, and has left behind safety and comfort for my sake. For these reasons I gave her my word never to leave her in danger or trouble. So where you take her, you must also take me, or suffer my severe displeasure."

"Oh, your majesty," and he knelt down. "Don't give such orders to a mere captain. Your father would have me—"

"I promise you I shall protect you," she told him. "Only you must obey me now. For I will not be forsworn on my promise. Nor is she to be chained, for she is too ill to resist you if she would. The carriage is being sent for us this morning. Convey us in that to prevent a public shame of the royalty. Then we will be at your service in the castle prison."

And so it was ordered that when the carriage arrived, its blinds were closed, and the Princess and the woman were taken up into it and driven to the castle in silence.

And when they arrived at the dungeons, wearing only their tattered clothing, and Rosalynn keeping her jewel hidden, they were taken into a cell. The woman was feverish and didn't seem to be aware of what was passing.

They set her on a pallet of straw, and at least the straw was clean, Rosalynn noticed. And when food was brought, it wasn't the common swill given to prisoners but regular food. So at least it had been rumored that the Princess was back.

9
Things in their Proper Order

In the late afternoon the woman awoke and looked at the gray walls so narrowly surrounding them. She turned her head and looked into Rosalynn's eyes.

"You are still with me, my child?" she asked.

"Yes, mistress, exactly where I belong, in the place I promised so many days ago." And Rosalynn took the woman's hand in both of hers. "They had orders to imprison all who came across from Folger, and I could not stop them, for the order was given on pain of death." She bowed her head. "Forgive me," and she cried over the scarred hand.

"You have neither wronged nor failed me," the woman said. "Did I not tell you there would be opportunity for you to prove yourself in the way you so desired?"

"Did you know that if you came to land with me that this would happen?" Rosalynn asked her.

"I knew that the entire way was fraught with danger. From my cottage to the archway of this castle the danger could only grow worse. Yet I still have good faith that we will be preserved. Where has Herron gone?"

"To find my father."

"When he returns, we will be comforted; and when your father comes, all will be well again."

Then the woman sank back into sleep, and Rosalynn waited.

It soon became dark in the little cell. The one window was high and narrow so that most of the day the cell was gray and dank smelling, and night was very black. Not a glimmer of starlight shone in, and curious rustlings in the corners spoke of smaller visitors.

Rosalynn tried to shut out the squeakings and rustling of the rats, and after only a few minutes she had to fight to shut out the darkness. It was so very dark a person couldn't stand it for long. She could not see her fingers before her face. Then she groped along the straw bed and found the woman's hand again, and for a while she wasn't as frightened as she had been. She closed her eyes to squeeze out the darkness.

But when she became still, the rats grew bolder until as she dozed in her sitting position, one of them ran across her foot. She gasped and nearly shrieked but caught herself. Then she pulled her feet in tightly.

Through the long night she sat thus, until at last she convinced herself that the cell was becoming grayer, and though she still couldn't see her fingers before her face, she concluded that she could. Then she told herself that rats have to sleep sometime, and that since they were quieter, they were probably asleep.

So at last she huddled onto a corner of the straw with her back against the woman to protect her, or at least to feel like she was protecting her, and went to sleep.

A miserable morning dawned outside. Inside the cell, Rosalynn woke up and stretched. She washed her face and made herself tidy. Then she cared for the woman as best she could.

"At least I am with her," she said out loud to herself to break the awful silence in the stone cell.

Several hours later, after the cell had enjoyed its hour or two of sunshine and was turning gray and chilly again, Herron suddenly appeared at the cell door with the turnkey.

He swept inside and dropped on one knee by the woman's side. "Such treatment to the one who has saved the Princess and the kingdom!" he exclaimed. "Word came to me that she was imprisoned as a spy from Folger. I came quickly and sent urgent word to your father to come and look into things, but it may be a few days. He is so caught up in this miserable war!"

"Has Rigel sent the rest of his troops over yet?" Rosalynn asked anxiously.

"Nay. Say nothing of that matter until your father comes, Princess," he advised her. "For spies are everywhere who would warn Rigel. I myself did not dare even send word to the King in writing of what we did, for if we were found out by the enemy, they would not cross that way. All the hopes of Bracken lie on what we did, for the armies of Folger grievously outnumber us."

Rosalynn nodded. He looked at her, and his eyes softened. "You are worn out, Princess. It's a miserable homecoming."

"Do not tell me to leave her, Herron," she said.

"Nay, it is queenly for you to stay here, and I would not discourage faithfulness to your friend. I only said you look worn."

"It is wearing to be in a cell like this. Night is the worst," she agreed. "But I would rather be with her

here than on a throne by myself, knowing I had deserted my friend."

"It is hard for me to leave either of you," he told her.

"Nay, there is a war, and you must serve in it. No harm will come to us here. The guards are frightened of harboring the Princess down here. They leave us in peace and feed us well."

"Very well, my Princess. Let us hope your father comes soon and ends this miserable and unjust confinement."

Then he kissed her hand, looked longingly at both of them, bowed, and left with the turnkey.

The woman opened her eyes. "Has another day come, my child?"

"Yes," Rosalynn said. "Herron has just been here, and he promises that my father is on his way."

"I feel much stronger now."

"There is food on the plate."

"I think I could eat it if it isn't too vile," she said. "How is the fare in this inn?" And she smiled at her own joke.

"They are bringing us food from the soldiers' mess," Rosalynn told her. "It's good enough. They are afraid to treat the Princess as a common prisoner."

"Very well." She rested a little longer, then ate the food Rosalynn had saved from their breakfast. Then she drank long and deeply from the morning's water ration.

At last the woman sat up, and it seemed that every passing moment gave her strength back. They ate their next meal together, and the woman kept Rosalynn close to her side so that Rosalynn felt as safe and comfortable as she had felt in the thicket of the sunny forest, even though the cell became grayer and grayer as the afternoon passed.

"When all is well here, will you go back home?" she asked.

"Nay. By the King's grace I will live in Bracken. For I sought to educate and civilize some of Rigel's soldiers and perhaps keep back this wicked day by the counsel of his chiefs. But it has failed, and war has come."

"Are you sad to leave your cottage behind?" Rosalynn asked.

"No."

The long day passed away, and the cell became black—inky black with no torchlight, nothing. The darkness was oppressive, and the knowledge that she was barred in worried Rosalynn as it had not done the night before.

The woman seemed calm, but she sensed Rosalynn's fear. As the rustlings in the corners started, Rosalynn shuddered and pulled her feet in. "They are worse than the wolves ever were!" she exclaimed fretfully.

She felt the woman's cloak as it was drawn around her and tucked under her feet. "Relax and sleep. It will pass the time more quickly," the woman said. And the Princess hung on to her words in the blackness of the cell.

"I'm afraid," she said in a small voice.

"Well, then, I'll tell you stories, and you can close your eyes and pretend you see them."

So the woman told her stories. And everything else in the vast prison was silent.

When the blackness was gray, Rosalynn woke up to the sound of hard boots tramping down toward their cell. She looked up and felt her heart beating hard. She was in no danger, but she feared for the woman. But in the next minute a bearded man with no sword was unlocking the cell door, and suddenly Rosalynn knew him. It was her father.

She flung herself into his arms.

"Why are you in this hole?" he asked. "What blackheart put you here after all your suffering?" And he wept over her.

"No, Father, I ordered the captain to do it, for he was bound to put my friend in prison, and I was bound to stay with her. I bound myself to stay with her."

But he was only half listening as he picked her up and kissed her. "You have grown up, my little girl. I see it in your eyes. You have seen the tragedy of my faithful Reynald and all that worthy band! Oh, that we had watched for the enemy more vigilantly!"

A shadow passed over her face when he mentioned Reynald and the others. "Is it true, then?" she asked. "Did they all die, Father?"

"Most," he said. "And this very day Rigel will march across the Bridge and take the rest of us, unless we fight beyond the ability of men."

"Nay," she said. "He will not have the victory today."

"You are a hopeful creature," he told her soberly.

"Father, this woman, unjustly imprisoned, has rescued me from death several times over," Rosalynn said as he set her down. "Release her, I beg you, for she is your friend and has been ere the war started."

The King started a little when he looked at the woman. "Pardon me," he said, "but I see you are not of Folger, as I was told."

"Nay. I come from the north," she said. And the King, knowing nothing else to do, kissed her hand in courteous greeting.

"I beg your pardon, madam. This grievous error shall be set right. My heart is indebted to you for bringing my daughter to me, even on this fateful day. Please come with me, and all shall be set right."

"The Princess is right about the battle today," the woman said. "Rigel shall not have the victory. I know that even now he assembles his men for a pompous march across the Bridge, and they shall be stopped on the Bridge."

"No more." He waved it away as a man does when he has too many cares to listen anymore. "Come, let us leave this place. I must rally the men at hand and then ride out in the afternoon."

Both Princess and woman exchanged glances, but the woman's eyes bade the Princess not to argue with him. Soon enough he would know the truth.

In the early afternoon of the same day, Herron came bounding into the great hall. His hair had been cut, and he was back in the familiar green leggings, shirt, and cowl of a rider. Except for the scars on his face, he was the same Herron as before.

"O King!" he cried at sight of Rosalynn's father on his throne, reviewing the maps of the battle plans. He threw himself to one knee on the carpet before the throne and flung his head up with the exultation and joy of a young and reckless colt.

"Quickly, my son, for before the hour ends, I must be at war," the King said.

Herron ducked his head in submission, then looked up in surprise. "Why, your majesty, has no one foretold it to you? What have the woman and Rosalynn been about?" But before he could wait for an answer, he exclaimed, "The Bridge has fallen! The Bridge has fallen! And Rigel and his men are undone. For they were on it, ten abreast, in ranks so deep as to blot out the sun! Coming to destroy our fair land and put us to the sword. The cables could not support the swaying as they marched in step, and it has collapsed!"

Then he leaped to his feet, drew his new sword, brandished it, and gave a shout of joy. "Am I truly the first to tell your majesty? Such is the speed of the King's riders! But why did the Princess not tell you?" he asked.

The King had started from his throne as though in pain, then he sank back and motioned to a page. "Call them," he gasped. "Call the woman and the girl!"

Moments later, the woman and Rosalynn hurried in. The woman knelt, then rose before the King.

"What had you been trying to tell me this morning?" the King asked. "For I brushed you away then, but now I see it was the truth."

"Aye," the woman said.

"We spoke the truth, Father," Rosalynn told him, coming up to him and putting her hand on his brawny knee. "For the wise woman knew the truth of the guards' secret song that told us how to destroy the Bridge. We went by night, and Herron climbed up and destroyed a wooden pin that helped anchor a crossbeam that held the main cables of one section of the Bridge."

"And it was so, even as you said." The King leaped up, recovered from the shock. His eyes fell on Herron, who stood poised and ready for orders. "Then the time has come for a rout of the enemy. Come, Herron!"

And they fled to the courtyard.

A person might expect battles to be exciting, but for Rosalynn, the next three days passed drearily enough. They were rainy and gray, and the entire war was pushing farther and farther north as the King of Bracken regained his territory.

The reports were good, and casualties for Bracken were slight. The two names that headed the list for valor were those of the King himself and his able soldier, Herron the Rider. At last the enemy soldiers were pushed to surrender. Within a week, the King was back with his daughter at the castle of the Duke of Small. Herron came with him and ate at his table.

"He personally battled the new leader of the Folger army," Herron said in a confidential whisper to the woman and Rosalynn. "Fellow named Varger, and it was hammer and tongs for a good while—only that Varger was a good fifteen years younger than his majesty. At last the King got one or two in on him, and yelled, 'Yield!' and Varger yelled back, 'No, I shall die like a man, not a prisoner!' And he took a mighty blow at the King that would have knocked a horse down, but the King parried it, finished him off, and then—"

"Enough Herron, enough," the King said, coming back to his meal from a small consultation with the steward about the feast to be held that night. "Let bards sing of deeds done on the field of battle. For men, the time has come to rebuild this little land. There is much to do, and after the festivities we shall be busy, the both of us, for my heart approves you too much to let you go back to being a courier."

He turned to the woman. "And you, madam—the time has been brief for me to confer with you; yet it is in my heart to speak with you at some length tonight. You must join me, the Duke, my daughter, and this young jackrabbit at our table."

"Of course, your majesty," she told him.

There was much to be done for the evening's celebration, and the castle was scrubbed and scoured and sanded and set alight with blazing candles in every window. After that, there were long speeches, and deeds of reparations given to peasants and yeomen who had lost lands, crops, and livestock in the war.

After that the people sat down to eat at tables that overflowed the great hall into the courtyard where the evening air was fresh and warm.

"May I escort you to our table?" the King asked the woman.

"Aye, your majesty."

"Only wait," he asked her as Herron leaned down to take the young Princess's arm. "My courtiers and family desire to know you better, somewhat. Are you a noble lady in your land to the north? We call your country the Diamond Isles, and precious little do we know of it."

"A fitting name enough. We call it the land of the morning dew, and yes, I am of a noble family." And on this she put her fingers to her collar, and from it drew out a jewel on a chain, and the jewel was an exact copy of Rosalynn's jewel.

Herron gasped. "And have I been so bold and friendly with a queen?" he asked, shocked at himself. "Every word she said bespoke her queenliness!"

"And I have treated her as a commoner," the King said. He bowed. "Forgive me, for the boy is right. You are every part a queen."

"For the boy's part, he was loyal and faithful and treated me as a queen, not knowing I was one, and for you, you were courteous and generous, your majesty."

Then he took her arm and led her into the banqueting room. And that same night before the kingdom was rebuilt, the bards sang of the King's valor in battle and his kingly heart, and next they sang of Herron winning his spurs and of his help in the destruction of the Bridge.

That same night Herron was knighted before all the nobles and ladies, and lands were given to him that made him one of the most powerful knights in the realm of Bracken. But his sole desire was still to serve the Princess, and so he won his greatest fame as a counselor, and from the combined wisdom of Rosalynn and Herron, peace and trade were established with Folger. The people there were taught trades that would not tax their wild land so that they traded with many nations.

As for the woman, she married the King and became mother to the Princess Rosalynn, and it is hard to say who loved each other more in that royal household. After the Princess was grown, Herron married her and spent his life serving her as he had always wanted to do, and she became a wise woman like her stepmother, showing off her royal jewels rarely, but more often displaying her queenly wisdom and gentleness to all people.